The
Underground
Skipper

Other books by William Campbell Gault

The Underground Skipper

William Campbell Gault

E. P. Dutton & Co., Inc.   New York

LIBRARY OF CONGRESS CATALOGING IN PUBLICATION DATA

Gault, William Campbell   The underground skipper

SUMMARY: The manager of a pro-baseball team begins a
new season with doubts about the re-hiring of a pitcher
who some years earlier had been Rookie of the Year but
was an unemployed bush-leaguer at twenty-eight.

[1. Baseball—Fiction] I. Title.
PZ7.G233Un [Fic] 74-23769 ISBN 0-525-41843-1

Published simultaneously in Canada by Clarke,
Irwin & Company Limited, Toronto and Vancouver

Designed by Nancy Danahy
Printed in the U.S.A.   First Edition
10 9 8 7 6 5 4 3 2 1

for
Peter Amacher

1

It was a cold January morning, I remember, and I was sitting at the breakfast table, reading the sports pages and listening to my waffles and pork sausage digest, when Myrna said, "Jimmy's back in town."

Myrna is my wife. Has been for thirty-two years. "Jimmy who?" I asked.

"Look at me when you talk to me. How many Jimmys do you know?"

I looked at her over the top of the paper. "Three hundred and seven, at the last count. I hope you don't mean Mr. Nothing."

"I mean Jimmy Cavanaugh," she said. "I mean the man who went with your darling daughter for two years."

"Isn't she your daughter, too?"

"She is my cherished child," Myrna admitted. "What I meant was, I always figured it was enough to be a good parent. With you, it was different and still is."

I put the paper down. "Explain it to me, noted college graduate."

"You were a very heavy father, Mike. Jailer would be closer."

"It worked, didn't it?"

"What does that mean? What worked?"

"The all-seeing eye, the firm hand. She didn't marry Mr. Nothing, did she? She married Dr. Harvey Bennett, the third richest dentist in Passaic. She gave us two beautiful grandchildren and will probably give us more. Is that not better than having her tied up to Mr. Nothing?"

"Did Dr. Harvey Bennett ever pitch two no-hitters in one season?"

"He never tried, not being in that trade. Did he ever leave our daughter for a Hollywood starlet, all of whose talent was below the neck? Did good old Harve ever throw an empty whiskey bottle through the stained-glass window of St. Jude's Church? Of all the pitches Mr. Nothing made, that was undoubtedly his most famous."

"He was drinking then," Myrna said. "He isn't now. He's joined Alcoholics Anonymous."

"And where did you learn all this?"

"From Mary. Jimmy was out there for dinner two nights ago."

I stared at her. She stared back. I have stared at many two-hundred-pound athletes and they didn't stare back. But in thirty-two years, I could never intimidate Myrna.

"All day yesterday, you could have told me this," I said. She nodded.

"But you didn't. And there has to be a reason."

She took a deep breath, still staring me in the eye. "He wants to sign with the Titans. He's a free agent now, Mike."

"From free soul to free agent in ten years," I said. "I'll

2

tell you something, and listen good. The day he signs with the Titans is the day I open a gas station in Des Moines.''

She shook her head. ''You're a hard and unforgiving man, Michael Xavier Ryan.''

''I'm a manager,'' I explained. ''Managers are paid what I think is important money to field a team of competent performers. They are not paid to act as welfare agents for over-the-hill pitchers.''

''You think Jimmy's over the hill at *twenty-eight*?''

''Jimmy Cavanaugh,'' I told her, ''was over the hill at twenty-two. But he had built up enough publicity value to make him a drawing card in the minors. That's what kept him from honest labor through the last six years.''

''When he was eighteen,'' my persistent wife with the infallible memory said, ''he won the Rookie of the Year Award. In the next two years he won the MVP and the Cy Young. And right now, *today*, you can get him for peanuts.''

''And so can any hotel in New York that needs a doorman. Could we change the subject?''

''No. Where was your greatest weakness last year, Mike?''

''At the box office,'' I said.

She waited.

''In the bullpen,'' I admitted, finally. ''Myrna, stay out of my business.''

''*Our* business,'' she corrected me. ''Who first suggested Heinie Schultz? Who convinced you to stay with Perry Washington?''

I didn't answer. Everybody is an expert in my business. Sportswriters, TV and radio announcers, fans, umpires, all relatives. They are all experts. If you don't believe me, ask them.

''That is certainly an honorable way,'' I said, ''for an un-

3

employed bush-leaguer to worm his way into the Titan bullpen, by having dinner with my happily married daughter.''

"That isn't why Jimmy came to dinner. He and Mary have
always been friends. Even before they were—they were
sweethearts, they were friends.''

"That gives Mr. Nothing a total of one. It is sad for him
that his one friend does not manage the Titans. Let him find
his second friend among the many hotel managers in this
large city.''

"When you were assembled," she asked quietly, "was
there a strike in the compassion department?''

Too many people confuse sentiment with sentimentality.
Fans and sportswriters and TV announcers. I guess you could
say almost everybody in the world except baseball managers
makes that dumb mistake.

There is a line in the second greatest book ever written in
the American language, a book by a man named Mark Harris. It is a book about baseball, more or less, and the line is
about a player and it goes: *One million dollars of promise
worth two cents on delivery.*

That is the line for James Duffy Cavanaugh. One year out
of high school, one year of smart lawyer dickering, he signed
with the Cards for a $200,000 bonus. Five years later, he was
pitching in the Coast League. He steadily worked his way
down from there.

You can blame booze or women or cards or drugs or too
much money too soon. Most kids today like to blame their
parents. Didn't their parents have parents? Blame them. You
can blame your way back to Adam and Eve on that route.

Let me tell you something, mister—nobody or nothing
ever destroyed anybody without a *lot* of help from the de-
stroyee.

I finished the sports pages, knowing no more than when I

4

had opened the paper. I finished my coffee and went to get my sheepskin-lined corduroy coat. It was a cold day on the east side of Manhattan.

"Where now?" my observant wife asked.

"Heinie's. Where else?"

"Where you will fill your big stomach with heavy German food and dark German beer," she informed me, "and come home begging for Alka Seltzer. That is strange fare for an Irishman, Mr. Ryan!"

"Don't blame me," I said. "You're the unpaid scout who suggested Heinie in the first place."

The wind blew through the canyon and the lovely secretaries scurried along the chilled street in their bright winter colors (to misquote Mr. Irwin Shaw), and the cabbies snarled and the traffic boomed. You could feel it through the soles of your feet, coming up through the cold concrete, the pulse of this great city everybody claims to hate. Why were they all here then, the people that mattered?

Heinie's is not exactly a gourmet restaurant. I have been to many gourmet restaurants and none of their food tasted as good as Heinie's. Maybe that is because I am not a gourmet.

Actually, it was not only his food and his beer that lured me. Heinie is my third-base coach, and about the fourth best in the League at that. He is also my hitting instructor, where he is probably the absolute tops in the history of the game.

But his gin rummy? I have played a lot of it, coast to coast, and met very few who were worse at it than Heinie Schultz. And he doesn't even know how bad he is. How many do you find like that?

He has a low ceiling in his place and a lot of dark mahogany and autographed pictures of all the famous names on his walls, all the way back to Gehrig and the immortal Babe.

It was too early for the lunch trade; only the problem

5

drinkers were at the bar, mostly ex-newspapermen. I headed for the corner booth in the restaurant, where Heinie was adding up yesterday's gross. He is a very sharp man around a dollar—unless he has cards in his hand.

"You're early," he said.

"My apartment was full of bad news," I said. "I needed the air."

"Bad news? What bad news?"

"Jimmy Cavanaugh's in town."

"So—?"

"He had dinner with my daughter two nights ago."

"Alone?"

"Of course not! At her home, in the presence of her husband."

"So—?"

"He's got a yen to pitch for the Titans."

Heinie nodded his big head thoughtfully. "That's bad news. Wiltern was always high on Jimmy."

Mr. Charles Frederick Wiltern was the international playboy and bon vivant who owned the Titans. Except for income, he was Cavanaugh's spiritual twin.

Heinie chewed his lower lip. After a few seconds, he said, "If Wiltern suggests him, don't make an issue of it, Mike."

"No issue," I said. "I'm sure I can find work with another club."

Physically and vocally, Heinie is blunt. "After last year?" he asked.

We had finished fifth in our division last year. Mel King, my predecessor, the winningest manager in Titan history, had never finished lower than second.

"We had a lot of injuries last year," I said.

"Not the year before," he said.

6

We had finished third in the division the year before. I said nothing. We both knew this was the critical year.

"We've been in this business a long time, Mike," he went on. "We've argued a lot of contracts from both sides of the table. One thing we learned, you don't win the argument without ammunition. You talk tough when you're strong and shut up when you're weak."

"I am not very good at shutting up," I said.

"This might be the smart time to get in some practice on it," he told me.

A lot of sportswriters and ballplayers ate and drank here and Heinie has a big ear. It was possible he had overheard some things about my current status with the club that I wasn't likely to hear.

"It's too early to worry about Cavanaugh," he said. "Take off your mittens. I'll get the cards."

He took the records with him into his small office and came back with a deck of cards. We cut for deal, and he won. This happens about one out of seven times. It was a harbinger for the day.

Three draws, and he's got gin. One draw, and he goes down with two points.

"My day," he commented.

"This game is all luck," I explained. "The skill element in this game is less than one thousandth of one percent."

"No wonder you always win," he said. "Mike, cheer up! In two months, we will be going to spring training, starting our most successful season in the last three. We made some good trades this winter, Mike."

I had no comment.

"Both of us working in the game we love," he went on in his happy winner's way. "What more can we ask?"

7

"Both of us working in the game we love," I admitted, "and one of us with a successful restaurant to fall back on. But what if the game I love stops loving me? What do I do then?"

"You're fifty-eight," he said. "You must have saved a few dollars."

"I'm fifty-seven," I corrected him. "I won't be fifty-eight until Friday."

"Gin," he said, laying down his cards.

At fifty-eight, it is not easy to get used to the sight of hair dryers in the locker room. It is not easy to hear players half a grade above average call eighty thousand dollars a year slave wages. It is not easy to hear punks laugh when you talk about curfew. Maybe nothing's easy when you're fifty-eight.

But what work can a middle-aged man find? There are German restaurants and Swedish restaurants, French, Italian, Armenian, soul food, and kosher. Have you ever heard of an Irish restaurant? And if I like Des Moines, where I was born, would I have left it before I finished high school? And what did I know about gas stations?

At sixteen, I was a starting catcher in the Appalachian League. At twenty, I was the same at Boston, hitting .306 my first full season in the big time. At thirty-eight, I was in the Titan farm system, managing. All the way up to Newark, and now here, on a three-year contract, this being the third.

Sure, I had put away a few dollars. My natural parsimony and Myrna's sharp eye for bargains had arranged that. Nelson Rockefeller had a few dollars, too. Had he retired? Who wants to die in Sun City? I'd rather be killed by a foul ball.

Heinie had won every hand and was almost a dollar and a half ahead when he had to quit to greet his luncheon trade. We do not play for large stakes.

I could have stayed for lunch and got my regular discount,

and maybe won my money back after lunch, but I was rest-less. I went out into the cold day and walked between all the hurrying people and looked at all the tall buildings, like a dumb kid from Des Moines, which I will probably always be.

Here I was, fifty-eight on the outside and still sixteen on the inside. And I wondered, when you finally lose The Big One, as everybody does, and they lay you out there in your best dark suit, will you still be sixteen inside?

It takes four thousand years to get to be sixteen—and twenty minutes later you are fifty-eight. Eighteen of those years I had played major league ball and enjoyed every second of it. Seventeen of those years I had managed minor league teams, hoping to get back with the big boys, expecting it less every year.

And then Mel King had retired. I suppose, if Mel hadn't been there, I might have. Any other farm system, I'd have been back to the big time, managing, much earlier. But Mel was another Connie Mack, another John McGraw, the best in his business.

I'd had some natural talent and worked hard to improve it. Lots of guys like me in this trade, some of them in the Hall of Fame. That's one of the reasons a kid like Jimmy Cava-naugh makes me burn inside. He had more than talent; he could have been another Koufax, another Spahn, if he'd put his mind to it.

Instead, at twenty-eight, he had tried to weasel his way into the Titan bullpen through his friendship with my daugh-ter.

There was no place else to go; I went home. Myrna had her bridge club over. I went into the den and tried to read. Not even Hemingway read good today. Maybe I'd read him too often.

9

Then Myrna stuck her head through the door and told me I had a phone call.

It was Charles Frederick Wiltern. "Are you busy, Mike? Could you drop over to the office for a few minutes?"

"I'll be there in fifteen," I told him.

It was only nine blocks; I walked. I could guess what he wanted to talk about and kept remembering Heinie's advice.

What I didn't expect is what I saw when his secretary ushered me into his fancy office. Mel King was sitting in the chair next to Wiltern's desk.

Mel got up when I walked in and smiled the best he knew how. "You're looking good, Mike."

There are three ages of man—young, middle-aged, and you're looking good.

I shook his hand and said, "You're looking pretty sound yourself. Thinking of coming out of retirement, Mel?"

He grinned. "Same old paranoia, huh? Nope. I'm happy where I am, up there in the wilds of Connecticut."

Our young owner beamed at both of us—rich punk kid, probably still on the sunny side of forty. "Mel's here for a purpose, Mike, and I'll state it frankly. You two like each other and respect each other. I'm not so insensitive that I don't realize neither one of you has ever been impressed by my judgment. But Mel agrees with me, this time, and that's why he's here. Sit down, Mike, and we'll talk."

I sat down and said, "We'll talk about Jimmy Cavanaugh."

He nodded. Mel nodded.

I said, "The last year of a three-year contract is a bad time to argue with the boss."

Wiltern looked at me levelly. "Do you want to sign another three-year contract right here and now? I can have it ready in five minutes, and Mel can witness it."

10

"I'll wait until the end of the season," I said. "I like to earn my way."

"That's my Mike," Mel said. "The last of the free enterprisers."

Wiltern sighed and shook his head. "Why are all the good managers so ornery? Is it an occupational disease?"

"Any man who pays his way is ornery," Mel explained. "Your papa knew that."

Wiltern stiffened. I knew this kid almost as well as Mel, and we both knew it was dangerous to go too far with him. But Mel didn't need him anymore, and he had never liked him.

I said quietly, "My record with the Titans doesn't earn me the right to be called a good manager. About Jimmy Cavanaugh, I admit to a personal bias. He went with my daughter for two years and left her for one of those dumb Hollywood starlets."

"I didn't know that," Wiltern said softly.

"You could have asked me," Mel said. "I knew it."

Charles Frederick Wiltern stared at Mel and his voice was colder than the air outside. "I realize you don't work for me anymore, Mel. But you will either show me some respect or I will personally throw you the hell out of here."

Mel's smile was tight. "Now you're talking like your papa. I'll stay."

"Stay then, and state your piece," Wiltern said. "You can rave about my father all you want. Just remember I gave both of you a lot more voice in player selection than he ever did."

And he knew twenty times as much about baseball as you do, sonny, I thought. I asked, "When did you develop this sudden and unexplainable admiration for the playboy moundsman, Mr. King?"

"I caught him a couple of times this summer," Mel ex-

11

plained, "when I was fishing out in Wisconsin. He was playing with the Green Bay Pirates."

"I know the Green Bay Packers play against men," I said. "But that's football. Is it possible the Green Bay Pirates play against girls in bloomers?"

"What's a bloomer?" Wiltern asked.

Mel ignored him, smiling coolly at me. "A kid like you, Mike, questioning my judgment?"

Mel was sixty-six, and looked every minute of it. He shrugged and yawned.

I said, "I've got this bias, which I've mentioned. A man shouldn't make decisions from that frame of mind. Mr. Wiltern, you still own this club."

"Couldn't you call me Chuck?" he asked.

"I called your father Mr. Wiltern, and a couple of minutes ago, you earned the same respect. As for Mel King, only two or three people in the world know more about baseball than he does, maybe four. If he says Cavanaugh can help us, I'm ready to listen."

"He was almost off the sauce when I saw him," Mel said, "and he looked sharp to me, Mike. He hasn't got the same fireball, but he's learned to think. It's a cinch he won't cost you much, after Green Bay, and I'm positive he won't hurt you."

"Okay," I decided, "I'll take him. I think we can make a trade for Witherspoon with Baltimore. They like him and I could use one more seasoned infielder."

"I'll get right on it," Charles Frederick Wiltern promised.

12

2

When I went out again, it was snowing, a wet, slushy snow. The cabbies were ignoring everybody who looked like they made less than seventy-five thousand dollars a year. Casing me, how could they tell I made more than that? I walked home.

Myrna stared at my soaked shoes and sniffy nose and said, "Sometimes it is wiser to go first class, Mike. The years of denial are behind us."

"The fault lies elsewhere," I said. "Would you get me Des Moines on the phone? I want to dicker for a filling station."

"Jimmy's going to be a Titan! I'm so happy for him."

"I hope you will be as happy in October as you are in January. Is there any of that German lager left, or did the Goren addicts drink it all up?"

"There's beer left. But this is not the day for it. You put on some dry socks and your slippers and I'll brew you a cup

13

of tea. Then we can relax and you can tell me about your meeting with Mr. Wiltern.''

I drank the tea slowly, while the frost worked its way out of my bones, while I told her about the meeting, up-playing my part, down-playing theirs.

When I had finished, she said, ''Bart Witherspoon? I don't know, Mike. He was coming along, the last half of September. He looked strong, saving that last game against Boston.''

''He is a three hundred percent anti-Catholic,'' I explained. ''He always puts out extra against Boston. Against the other ten clubs, his record is very spotty.''

''I never realized that,'' she said.

''That is one of the reasons,'' I said, ''you are not the manager of the New York Titans. Could we forget baseball for the rest of this miserable day?''

It really hadn't been that bad a day. My manhood was restored; I had turned down a three-year contract. And after a fine steak dinner, Myrna decided she wanted to play some gin rummy with the expert. I won back all the money I had lost to Heinie, and thirty-five cents extra.

Friday night, Mary and Harve came to town with reservations at a fancy restaurant and tickets for a musical, their birthday present to me.

Harve was in the kitchen, fixing a faucet for Myrna, when Mary said to me quietly, ''Jimmy's really changed, Dad. Go easy on him, won't you?''

''If he delivers,'' I said. ''If he keeps his nose clean.''

''Oh, Dad—! Even before he turned crazy, you didn't like him, did you?''

''Before he went sour,'' I explained, ''he was a showboater. I have always taken a dim view of showboaters.''

''The Hall of Fame is full of them,'' she argued.

14

"Name me one who was washed up at twenty-two. What is it with you and this butterfly? You're a married woman, honey."

"Happily," she said. *"Very happily.* Jimmy is my friend, Dad, my good friend. And nothing more. Get that straight."

"So, okay. If your good friend delivers, he will have no problems with me. Let's not argue. It's my birthday. I'm crowding sixty, kid!"

She kissed me on the nose. "Happy birthday! And Daddy, this is one of the best restaurants in town we're going to. You're not going to order steak again, are you?"

"If there's anything else on the menu I can pronounce, I'll order it," I promised. "I could have got us a discount at Heinie's."

I couldn't pronounce what I ate. Mary (the college French major) ordered it for me. It wasn't bad, though mostly sauce. The musical was louder than it was good but it was still a hundred and thirteen percentage points above those weirdo modern dramas Myrna keeps dragging me to.

The sun came back next morning and the temperature went up and Heinie's brief winning streak came to an end. As long as I didn't have to look at Mr. Nothing, I could almost forget him. And I wouldn't have to look at him until March.

I thought.

The next Thursday, at noon, I was in our private booth, eating a liver sausage on dark rye while Heinie was out gladhanding the tourists, when Jimmy took the seat across from me.

"Hello, skipper," he said.

"You signed, huh?"

He nodded. "I can do you some good, Mr. Ryan. I mean it."

"You have already done me good," I said, "by not marrying my daughter. I am getting too old and too cynical to expect two favors in one lifetime from the same person."

"Okay. I just wanted you to know." He got up and walked away.

This was not the brash Jimmy I remembered. He looked thirty-five, or more. His voice was at least forty percent quieter, as were his clothes. His hair was long. But everybody on our club had long hair, except Heinie and me. It was possible we were the ones out of step.

Heinie came back from his good will mission, bringing a plate of sauerbraten along. "I was expecting an explosion over here," he said.

I said nothing.

"He's sure aged," Heinie said. "A lot quieter, too, isn't he?"

I nodded.

"Still handsome, though. He always was a handsome devil."

"Handsome is as handsome does," I said.

"Right, boss. Well, we'll see what he does, come March. Have we made that deal for Witherspoon yet?"

"Just about. We'll probably get Heilbraun."

"I hope we do. He's a real old pro. That's what we always needed at third, a heady, steady Kraut."

Mel had had Pete Pulaski at third, one of the best. And Mark Button at short, a man who'd won six Golden Gloves. They'd retired the same year Mel had, along with some other stars. I don't want to downgrade a genius, but Mel had left me a lot of holes.

I still had Joe Valdez at second and Chris Oliver at first, both well above average. The left side of the infield had been our problem. Carl Heilbraun should have a few good years in

16

him. And that kid shortstop, Al Ward, had looked flashy when I'd brought him up from Oil City last September.

So what do you do? You take the best available boys you can assemble and get them into condition and try to teach them to make fewer bonehead plays than the national average. You trust your luck and the instincts you should have developed through forty-two years of play-for-pay ball and hope for the best.

If it works, another year of glory is ahead. It if doesn't work, you settle down at some dopey retirement village and play golf and bore your neighbors blind with exciting stories of your illustrious career.

I didn't play golf. I didn't play tennis. I didn't hunt, fish, bowl, pitch horseshoes, or collect stamps. What I did for recreation was play gin rummy, read books by American writers, and argue with Myrna. What I did to help me believe there was still a place for me in this world was manage the Titans.

I relieved Heinie of ninety-two cents and went home early, before his luck could change. There was a note from Myrna, explaining that Selvedge's had a sale on drapes and she was going to try to pick up a set for our bedroom. Five will get you seven, she'd come home with everything but drapes.

I dug out last year's scouting reports and took them into the den. I was putting together everything we had on Carl Heilbraun when the phone rang.

It was Bart Witherspoon. "Thanks a lot, skipper," he said.

"For what?"

"For repaying me for all those years of loyalty by trading me to the Orioles."

"They need relief pitching bad, Bart. And they *are* contenders. I had to make room for the man who broke my

17

daughter's heart. You can't think signing Jimmy Cavanaugh was *my* idea."

"Some story!" he said. "I was not born yesterday, skipper."

Maybe the day before? I thought. I said nothing.

"I have been a fool," he went on. "One thing I always believed, if there is one Roman Catholic who is almost human, it is Mike Ryan."

"There is no room for bigotry in baseball, Bart. And do not ever make that remark in a place where I can reach you. You are not so ugly that a rearrangement of your features would be an automatic improvement."

"You can talk real tough over the phone, old man."

"Name the place we can meet," I said. "I'll be there."

"Sure you will! And then I'd be blacklisted all over the League. Drop dead, Mike!" He hung up.

I would have to make sure our tender warriors had the ear flaps on their batting helmets if Baltimore brought Bart in against us. I made a note of it. With that designated hitter's ruling in our League, we would get no return chance to bounce one off his bean. It is a sissy ruling, eliminating the classic and traditional revenge motif from baseball.

Heilbraun looked sound on paper and from what I remembered about him. He would never make the Hall of Fame, but he would never give his manager any ulcers, either. That kid, that Al Ward, I was a little leary of. He had made some sensational plays—and blown some easy grounders, playing them lazy. He had always had at least three females waiting for him in the parking lot. One thing I didn't need was two Romeos on one club.

The days went by, getting no colder and no warmer, just going by. I lose track of days when they mean nothing, when you don't have to figure ahead for pitching rotation and dou-

18

bleheaders and like that. What I mean is, you can't fill your days with gin and rereading John Steinbeck.

All the public thought about, and the writers wrote about, was basketball, the Knicks. That is some game, where if you are not twelve feet tall, you are good only for selling pop at the refreshment stand. And football? Have you ever seen a professional football player whose head was thicker than his neck? Why don't they name those games what they are—freak shows? And hockey? If you want to look at Canadians, I say move to Canada.

But March came along, as it always did. Even after you are laid out in your best dark suit, March will come along. Unless we finally blow up this planet, as we seem to be heading for.

Myrna fussed and fussed, trying to get *exactly* the right people to sublet our apartment for a month, people who did not drink, smoke, eat, or sleep. She had to accompany us to spring training. How could we prepare for our summer battles without the brilliant analytical judgments of Myrna Mary O'Brien Ryan?

Titanville is on the east coast of Florida. It had been bought by Charles Frederick Wiltern's grandfather from a subdivision developer who had gone broke in 1928, when the Florida land boom had collapsed. The subdivider had called it Villa Leandro. Charles Frederick Wiltern the First had renamed it in the American language. He had bought up most of the other land around there at the same time, and grown even richer on the second Florida land boom.

We had the manager's apartment, of course—three bedrooms and three baths. I don't know how a man can take three baths at one time, but maybe Thorstein Veblen can explain it to you.

The sun was shining in Florida; it was the season of hope

19

again. The kids from the bushes were here, hoping that this was the year they would make the big step. The old pros would be here later, hoping that this was the year their arthritis would disappear. Every club is a winner before the season starts.

"Aren't you going to help me unpack?" Myrna asked.

"There are a couple of farm club managers I have to talk to," I explained, "and some kids I'd like to see work out. I'll unpack my stuff later."

"You're wearing ninety-two percent of your stuff," she said, "except for your uniform. We're going to eat out tonight, aren't we? I don't want to go grocery shopping."

"If you have enough of your grocery money left to buy me a decent steak, why not eat out? See you later."

The sun was bright and I could hear the chatter of the rookies and the crack of the bat as I turned into Wiltern Lane. It might be March to some people; it was the first of January to me. The new year started today.

The crack of the bat was Heinie's. He was chopping out grounders to the kid infielders and they were throwing them to second, first, or third, depending on the delayed call by Heinie.

He could certainly handle a bat, that man, even now. He could slice a grounder or hook it, give it top spin, back spin, or no spin. The delayed call gimmick had been my idea, testing reaction time.

An infielder has to decide where he's going to throw *before* the ball is hit—on most plays.

But how about surprise steals and runners with different speeds on the bases? I don't expect to sign any Einsteins. Brainy kids do not usually pick baseball as a career. If they couldn't think well, I wanted them to think fast.

The Oil City flash, Al Ward, was plainly the cream of the

20

lot, moving smoothly and quickly to either side, throwing arrows to any base.

Heinie gave the bat to Clem Pelt, our first-base coach, and came over to stand with me. "One hole is filled," he said.

"Ward?"

"Right. And if Heilbraun comes through at third—?"

"We will only have to compete with golf and tennis," I answered, "and the end of the basketball season and the start of the football season, and then the start of another basketball season."

"Attendance—is that all baseball means to you, Mike?"

I shook my head. "It is America I am worried about. They have turned to freak shows and sissy sports. They have deserted the immortal Babe for people like Bobby Riggs."

Heinie said nothing.

"Ward's bat," I said, "might be another possible plus. But what does .343 in the Texas League translate into in the big time?"

Heinie shrugged. "We shall have to wait and see. His swing looks sound to me. But against a major league pitcher?" He shrugged again. "Gin rummy tonight?"

"No. Not until next fall, after the Series, which we had better be in. From now until then, it is all business, Heinie."

"For you," he said. "For me, I intend to find somebody I can beat this summer. I don't like TV reruns. If that is mutiny, fire me—and lose your discount at my restaurant."

3

Myrna and I were sharing (75–25) a planked Chateaubriand at La Casa de Steak when The Man walked in.

"Jimmy!" my co-manager called. "Over here, Jimmy!"

He glanced doubtfully at me and walked slowly over. "Hello, Mrs. Ryan. You're certainly looking good."

"And you're as beautiful as ever," she said. "Sit down and tell me about your adventures."

He looked at me and around the room and wound up looking uncomfortable. "I'd love to," he said, "but I'm meeting some people. You're doing your hair differently now, aren't you? I like it."

"Thank you. You always know what to say, Jimmy."

There was a silence—which I filled. "You're down early."

"I can use the conditioning," he said. "A man doesn't stay too sharp pitching for the Green Bay Pirates."

A man who respects his trade does, I thought. I said nothing.

22

"Well," he said, "it was nice seeing you again, Mrs. Ryan. Give my regards to Mary." He went away.

"Isn't he handsome?" Myrna breathed. "You have to admit that, Mike."

"Handsome is as handsome does," I said.

She shook her head. "No. Handsome is as handsome is, an end in itself. Someday, somehow, you will have to find your way into the twentieth century, old man."

All my heroes were twentieth century people. All of my life had been spent in the twentieth century. If Myrna had majored in history instead of art at NYU, she would realize that the cream of the twentieth century was the first half of it. Except for DiMaggio, Mantle, and Mark Harris. Okay— Mays, Koufax, Spahn, Robinson, Musial, too. And probably some others I've overlooked. She might have a point, at that. . . .

I had breakfast with the Oil City skipper, Pete Pulaski, next morning. "I wanted to talk about Al Ward," I explained. "When he was up with us those couple of weeks in September, I didn't use him much."

"You should have," Pete said. "You might have climbed up to fourth place. He's ready, Mike. He's got everything Mark Button had when Mark was his age."

"Mark was no ladies' man," I pointed out.

"Mark had a lot of bluenose hangups," Pete said. "I figure a player's private life is not a manager's business."

"When a player's private life interferes with his performance on the field, it had better be a manager's business. You sure eat fast."

"You're buying," he explained, "so I'm shoveling." He beckoned the waitress. "Another stack of cakes, please, and some more sausage."

23

"How about your other infielders?" I asked. "How about that Caravelli?"

He shook his head. "Not this year, not yet."

"You need him, maybe, huh?"

"You are a mistrusting man, Mike. You think I don't need Ward?"

"I am not, by nature, mistrusting. It is the times, Pete. Has this Ward any girl friend he favors above the others?"

"I never asked him. That was a smart move you made, picking up Cavanaugh. I'll bet you got him cheap."

"Not as cheap as Green Bay did. My smartest move was getting Heilbraun. He plays third like you used to."

"He must play it better," Pete said. "He's the same age I am, and he's still up there."

"He stayed in shape," I explained. "He curbed his appetite."

The sun kept shining and the ache in my right knee went away. Gus Filcher of the Tigers had messed up the cartilage in that knee twenty-six years ago, trying to come home from third on a short fly ball. They had carried us both off on stretchers.

A couple of days after my breakfast with Pulaski, I was watching batting practice when who should be standing next to me but Button, my second favorite Mark, after Harris.

"You're looking good, Mike," he said.

"So I've been told. How are things out in cuckoo land?"

He was now our scout in California. He shrugged. "Okay. At least we don't have this sweltering heat."

It was 74 degrees, with a light breeze. I asked, "Had a look at Al Ward yet?"

"I signed him. He can do it for you."

"The way I hear it, he's a swinger."

24

Mark smiled. "Not for long, not under you. Don't crowd him, though, Mike. He's his own man."

Pulaski and Button were not likely to be wrong about infielders. Or much else. One of them would some day have my job, for sure. If he was patient.

Heilbraun was a comfort, always in condition, a little slower than his best days, making up for it with his noodle, with a book on every hitter in the League, playing them where it hurt them the most.

We had only one ace left from Mel's great pitching staff, Elmer Spack. The others were sound, but by no means stars. I wouldn't have to lose the bat of Willie Washington, last year's third baseman. He could go back to right field, where he was happiest. The man who had finished the season for us at shortstop, Kermit Davis, was too dumb for the action there. He was still a good choice for designated hitter.

I ran them through my mind, man by man, and figured we should do better this year. Better was not enough. We had finished fifth in a six-team division; fourth would be better than fifth. I was not aiming for fourth.

"We are stronger in every department," Myrna informed me at dinner one night. "And getting rid of Bart Witherspoon helped. He cost you some important ball games, Mike."

"That is a radical change from your January evaluation of him," I said.

"I didn't know he was a bigot then," she explained. "We need another starting pitcher, Mike."

"I know, I know! I've been looking for one."

"You could use Jimmy as a starter," she said thoughtfully, "and pick up Tom Balding for the bullpen. The Angels are about ready to release him."

25

"And where did you pick up that startling piece of information?"

"From Jane Button. I saw her in the supermarket this morning. Mark certainly found himself a wonderful wife—finally."

"He waited for Miss Right, just as our daughter waited for Mr. Right. I have other plans for Jimmy, such as ticket promotion or hot dog vending. As for Tom Balding, he has finally lived up to his name; he is balding. He must be fifty years old!"

"He won't even be thirty-three until May," Myrna said, "and he is very bitter about the Angels."

"Myrna, how many times must I tell you to stay out of my business?"

"As soon as the season starts," she promised, "I will ease off. But you think about that Tom Balding."

"Huh!" I said.

I waited until she had left for her nightly bridge game before phoning Clem Pelt. Clem lived in California in the off season and played a lot of golf with athletes. "Call a few of your friends in cuckoo land," I told him, "and get the word on Tom Balding. I hear he is very unhappy with the Angels."

"I played golf with him in January," Clem told me, "and he didn't seem unhappy to me. Where'd you get that story?"

"I have my sources. Just do the phoning, Clem. I'll do the thinking."

I got out the Angel book and read the page on Balding. He had saved 12 games last year, won 6, lost 2. He had an earned run average of 2.93. He would be thirty-three in May. His lifetime era was 2.74, his lifetime won-lost record impressive.

It had to be a silly supermarket rumor; the Angels wouldn't

give up this man, not at any price we could afford in money or players.

Unless something had happened to his arm over the winter? That wouldn't be in the book and certainly wouldn't be broadcast by the Angel publicity department. Clem would no doubt ask his golfing friends about that.

He reported back after breakfast next morning. "Tom cracked up his car last November," he told me. "The Angels think his arm was damaged. Tom's playing it cute, I guess. He doesn't argue with 'em."

"Maybe he wants to leave the Golden State. What do you think, Clem?"

"If he's got a bad arm, he's the longest bad-armed golfer in America. He was thirty yards past me off every tee. You're right, though, he hates California for some dumb reason."

"Call some more friends," I said. "Get the word. But don't call Tom. He's got a *big* mouth."

"I will handle it with my usual finesse," Clem assured me.

We would play our first exhibition game tomorrow, against the Braves. That is normally a time to try out rookies, but they had been tried through the intra-squad games—and found wanting. There was a lot of potential ivory in our farm clubs. The best of them, except for Ward, were still at least one year short of major league standards. And I had this tentative starting lineup I wanted to test.

I asked Red Murphy, our pitching coach, what he thought about Cavanaugh as a starter.

He shrugged. "Maybe. He's certainly working hard. And I guess he's straightened out his private life, too. I see him at early mass. That's when the *good* Catholics congregate, Mike."

27

I preferred the eleven o'clock service myself, but did not rise to the bait. I said, "I also hear he is out with a different young lovely every evening."

"If I were single," Red said, "and twenty-eight years old and had his looks, I would follow his example on that."

"Let's get back to baseball."

"Okay. After Spack, he might be your best pitcher. But whether he's got the stamina left to be a starter—? We'll have to wait and see."

"We'll start him against the Braves," I decided. "He'll go the full three innings—unless the roof caves in." I paused. "You were with Detroit when Balding was, weren't you?"

"Sure was. Tom and I, together, won thirty-nine games for them in '68." He looked at me doubtfully. "Something cooking?"

"Just an idea I had. Mum's the word, Red."

He nodded. "How about that accident he had last November?"

"It probably ruined his arm. I repeat, mum is the word."

The Braves had harvested a bumper crop of rookies from their farm clubs last spring and had been a contender all season in that other league. Youth had lost them a few key games in the stretch run; they had patched the holes with winter trades. They figured this was *their* year.

They still had the greatest player in this half of the century, Mr. Henry Aaron. On the field and at the box office, no club had anybody to match him.

They were still trying out a few rookies when we went up against them next afternoon. Cavanaugh disposed of two of them without much trouble—and Bad Henry stepped up to the plate.

This was the year he was slated to break Babe Ruth's

28

home run record, so there were a few jeers mixed in among the cheers from the stands. Some people won't let a man die.

Henry took one outside low for a ball, and then two real cuties for strikes, showing no emotion, which is his way. Golden Jimmy should have wasted one now, but he'd always had more vanity than sense. He shook off the catcher's call and tried to blaze one.

The ball went out, over the fence, over the palm trees, heading for the ocean, barely missing a fishing boat a few miles off shore.

I went out to the mound. Jimmy waited for me, his face stiff.

I said, "You are no longer eighteen and the toast of St. Louis."

"I am well aware of that, Mr. Ryan. I figured it was better to try my fastball, now, when it can't hurt us. Then I'll know, when it matters, if I still have it."

"If you wanted to know, you should have asked me. Speed is not your forte anymore. Fastballs to Henry Aaron is what headed him for the Hall of Fame, and sent quite a few pitchers into other lines of work."

He said nothing.

I said, "I have been seriously considering you as a starter. But the ultimate decision will have to depend on you."

He nodded, his face cold, his eyes hot.

The next man fouled them out of the inning and we opened with Valdez, the smartest bat on the club. Oliver would follow him, and then Kermit Davis, our new designated hitter.

Davis was not happy about his new slot, explaining to Heinie that if his glove had been good enough to play short-stop last year, it should certainly still be good enough for the

29

outfield this year. Heinie had not explained back the obvious to him; his glove had *not* been good enough at shortstop last year, nor had his brain.

Valdez walked, after fouling off about half a dozen, and Oliver sacrificed him to second. Kermit came up and hit the first pitch out of the park and we led, 2 to 1.

Cavanaugh went the full three, giving up two more hits and one walk, but no runs. We still led, 2 to 1, when Spack opened the fourth.

Elmer Everett Spack—there is a man I enjoy watching at his trade, an M.A. from Columbia, though you would never know it to look at him, with his straw hair and buck teeth. He *thinks* before he throws, and he thinks better than 99 percent of the batters in the League. He is another Koufax, except for being a Gentile and right-handed.

He took us through the next three innings with one hit and no walks and Cal Every, one of our winter trades, came in to pitch the last three.

He got into trouble right away, no fault of his. Ward blew an easy grounder and senile blindness behind the plate on what was clearly a third strike put two men on with nobody out.

Cal fought his way out of it against the heart of the order, striking out Carty with men on second and third.

From her box seat above the dugout, Myrna said, "We are solid, Mike. This could be the year."

I didn't turn around.

"Jimmy still has his fastball," she went on, "despite what Henry did to it. There aren't many Aarons around, Mike."

I pretended not to hear.

"She could be right," Heinie said.

"Bridge is her game," I said. "We will stick with baseball. You're overdue in the third-base coaching box."

30

We had two out in the ninth, the score still 2 to 1, when Ward blew another, playing the ball as a routine out when the man racing to first was Garr, their speedster.

Then Carty came up and belted one. Only a great leap by Otis Paige, in center field, kept the Braves from taking the lead. Otis caught the ball three feet above the fence and heading for downtown. Our game, 2 to 1.

I told Heinie, "I want to see Ward in my office—*before* his shower."

He was there before I was, a slim, handsome kid, with baby blue eyes and blond hair almost down to his shoulders. He didn't look scared.

"Two dumb plays in one game," I said, "could keep you in Oil City the rest of your life."

He said nothing, looking at me steadily.

"You may talk," I said.

"What's to say, skipper? The first one I blew. The second one, I had no idea Garr was that fast."

"You were not told or have never read that Garr was fast?"

"I knew it. I didn't think *anybody* was that fast."

"You have a loose and easy way of playing that disturbs me," I said. "I realize baseball is a game, but it is a serious game, like life."

"I've been watching shortstops all my life," he said. "The great ones I've watched played it loose and easy."

"On the outside," I explained to him patiently, "they are loose and easy. On the inside, they are cold and calculating hustlers."

He nodded.

"That is your sermon for today," I said. "We will discuss your social life at another time. You may go."

He didn't go. He stood there, still not scared.

31

"Speak your mind," I said.

"There's a thing I've always believed," he said. "So long as I don't break training, I've always figured my social life is nobody's business but mine."

"Unless it interferes with your performance on the field."

"That, of course," he said, "is a judgment only you can make." He turned and went out.

Feisty kid, bullheaded. But my message had gone through, I was sure. And now for Myrna.

She was slicing tomatoes for a salad when I came into the kitchen. "Good ball game," she commented.

"You are cutting those tomatoes at the wrong angle," I said, "and you have trimmed too much fat from this steak. Any expert knows the only flavor in meat is in the fat."

"Don't try to be subtle, Mike. It's not your way. I shouldn't have spoken up as I did in front of the others. I've never done it before. I'll never do it again, publicly or privately."

"Privately is okay," I said, "occasionally. You have a sharp eye, Mrs. Ryan. And I will never forget you suggested Heinie Schultz. He could be a source of pocket money for me through the twilight years."

"From now on," she said "there will be no baseball advice from me in our house—unless I am asked."

"Fair enough. Could I have a kiss?"

She kissed me and patted my cheek and sighed. "Neither one of us would be worth much on a trade. We'd better be nice to each other."

4

I stopped taking the antacid pills after the Braves game. We were not bad. We had really made only one definite error in that exhibition opener; Garr might have beaten *any* throw to first with his speed.

And the word from California was promising. Balding was unhappy. After a phone call from me, C. F. Wiltern sent out some feelers in his indirect way. We had a couple of outfielders at Syracuse the Angels had tried to dicker for in February; Wiltern opened with them, hoping the Angels would be the first to suggest Balding.

My tentative starting lineup shaped up like this:

Joe Valdez 2b   Carl Heilbraun 3b
Chris Oliver 1b   Perry Washington lf
Kermit Davis dh   Al Ward ss
Otis Paige cf   Luther Locust c
Willie Washington rf

There would be very few changes against right-handers; my important boys were switch hitters. Ward was near the bottom only because he was new to big league pitching. He could work his way up. He'd led the Texas League with his bat at Oil City.

Luther Locust, our first-string catcher, usually hit around the .200 mark, but was good for sixteen or eighteen homers a year. It is comfortable to have a man at the bottom of your batting order who's treated with respect by opposing pitchers.

We went down the coast to play the Dodgers Thursday. If the climate is so wonderful in cuckoo land, why do the Los Angeles Dodgers train in Florida? How could anybody with sense desert Brooklyn, a borough of New York? There are many unanswerable questions in baseball.

Most of the writers had picked them to take the Western Division crown in the National League this year. Trusting the prophecies of baseball writers is a sure way to wind up on welfare, but I was inclined to agree with them this time. It was a solid club, on paper.

They, like the Braves, were still trying out rookies, and the senior citizen of our pitching staff, Jess Lepert, handled them with ease—nine up, nine down. That Jess, he was another Spahn, ageless and invincible at thirty-seven.

In the fourth inning, they brought in the regulars. I decided to stick with Jess for another inning, one of my rare mistakes. When the smoke cleared, it was Dodgers 5, Titans 1.

"Myrna should have come down for this game," Heinie kidded me. "We needed her."

"Let's leave the humor to Bob Hope," I suggested.

Davis, Paige, and Willie Washington all got on to open the fifth. Heilbraun brought two of them home with a long single to right field and Perry Washington blasted one over the fence to put us ahead again.

I will not bore you with the details of that ridiculous game. We lost it in the ninth, 17 to 16.

On the bus going home, Heinie said, "One thing today taught us, we have power at the plate."

"The lesson we learned," I corrected him, "is what we knew all last year. Our bullpen is weak."

"And Jess is only good for three innings."

"In March. In July, when his blood begins to circulate, he will return to normal. Heinie, if we get bullpen help, I have a feeling we will head right for the top."

And where would we find bullpen help? Balding, maybe. That was only one man. Off his record, he could be our long reliever. But who could we bring in for one inning, or one batter? Who could be our spot and short relievers?

The days of the nine-inning pitcher were long gone. Pennants were won in the bullpen in this decadent half of the century.

At home, Myrna was trying to figure out a bridge hand in the paper. "How'd you do?" she asked, without looking up.

"We lost by one run, with two out in the ninth."

"I blew a laydown grand slam," she informed me, "doubled and redoubled. Tomorrow just has to be better for both of us."

Had she left the club? After thirty-two years, had she deserted me? I asked, "What's for dinner?"

"It's in the oven," she said. "Tuna fish casserole. There's a letter from Mary on the coffee table."

After this so-called dinner, we watched the news together on the tube—until the sports came on. Then Myrna went out to put the dishes in the dishwasher. That move was too obvious; she was disciplining me. Two could play that game.

Later, she watched a movie on the tube while I checked the rosters of every club in both leagues and then on to every pitcher they owned all the way down to Double-A ball. Nothing. Red would have to improve what we had.

I was probably over-worrying, an early sign of senility. Which club was perfect? What club ever had been? We had hitting and fielding and sound starting pitchers. We were as close to perfect as any of the other clubs in the division. Was I beginning to doubt my own proven managerial ability?

Just before lunch next morning, Bugs Erp, our trainer, came out to tell me I had a long-distance phone call.

It was Wiltern. "Tom Balding is on a plane, heading your way," he informed me. "What happened yesterday? Seventeen runs!"

"We had sixteen," I reminded him. "If Balding had been here, we could have held 'em to fourteen and won by two. It was just one of those days."

"Balding should round us out, don't you think?"

"Almost," I agreed. "I could use a seasoned short reliever, but I spent three hours last night poring over rosters and couldn't find one likely to be available. Murphy will have to mold us one."

"Sure. Well, I'm off to Europe for a few months. Luck, Mike."

Off to Europe. . . . He wouldn't even be here for opening day. His father had missed about four home games a year, and spent the off season scouring the country for talent.

But he was not a stingy owner, as owners go. And he was not vindictive, sticking with Mel, knowing the man had no respect for him. I'll have to admit his worst fault was not believing the world is a stitched horsehide ball.

Balding hit town around four; I saw him in my office at four-thirty.

"The arm?" I asked. "The straight truth, Tom."

He smiled. "Don't you read the papers, Mike?"

36

I stared at him, saying nothing.

"I was born in Brooklyn," he said, "and grew up there and intend to die there. Detroit was not too far, nor Boston. But California, that's a whole other country."

"I know. Are you telling me your arm is sound?"

"My arm," he said, in his modest way, "could possibly put you into the World Series."

"Okay. No more need be said. Check in with Red Murphy. He'll get you settled and uniformed."

I went home feeling better. Myrna was working a crossword puzzle. "What's for dinner?" I asked.

"Macaroni and cheese," she said. "It's in the oven."

The war was still on. "We signed Balding," I said.

"Balding who?"

I sat down across the table from her. "I surrender. Let's discuss an exchange of prisoners."

She looked up and smiled. "Mike, I'm not fighting you. I just finally realized what you have been saying all these years is true. I should stay out of your business."

"And the tuna fish casserole, followed by macaroni and cheese, that was only a coincidence?"

She shook her head. "It was shoddy domestic petulance. It will end tonight. Mike, I love you. And I think you are the ablest manager in either league. You have enough critics and pseudo-experts sniping at you. You certainly deserve some peace at home."

"Put the macaroni in the icebox," I said. "We're going out for a steak. On me."

The Dodgers came up to Titanville next day for more fun and games. There was not much fun in the game for them, hitting into two double plays in the first three innings, having Joshua picked off at second. We had us an infield.

In the ninth, Every weakened and Balding came in with

37

runners on first and third and only one out. Two palm balls, a slider, and a blazer took care of one man. An infield pop-up ended the game, ours, 2–0.

A man can dream big in the spring. Climbing from fifth in the division to the World Series might be too big a dream, even for March, but there was no resemblance between this team and last year's. The dream lasted all through the grapefruit run and was still alive and kicking when we boarded the plane for New York.

We would open against Baltimore, at home, and we would be ready. Rusty Jones, of *The Times,* the only newspaper writer I could read as a regular diet, worded it better than I can in his column:

> The Iowa Sage has done it again. Who but Michael Xavier Ryan had the perception to realize Jimmy Cavanaugh was not over the hill; that all he ever lacked was drying out? Who else would have come up with the one man the Titans needed to bolster the bullpen, and then conned the Angels out of Tom Balding? And Carl Heilbraun? He has been around a long time and will continue to be around a long time.
>
> Buried in Newark through those years Mel King reigned, the luster of the present Titan skipper was shrouded by the bushes. It is heartening to see him finally come into his own. . . .

Mel came down from Connecticut for the opener and had dinner with us the night before.

"I kept looking for your disclaimer in *The Times,*" he said, "but it never showed. I mean, Rusty Jones giving *you* credit for signing Jimmy Cavanaugh?"

"I don't recall the piece," I said. "Considering the vicious things some of the other writers have said about me, an error in my favor is due."

"I'll buy that. We still need a short reliever, Mike."

38

"I know. But from where? The Green Bay Pirates?"

Something flickered in Myrna's eyes, but she only said, "More potatoes, Mel?"

She stayed with her new image through dinner. Mel and I talked mostly baseball, Mel not being a reader. She showed wifely interest and laughed at Mel's dumb jokes and never once intruded her own opinion—the perfect wife, the gracious hostess.

At breakfast, I said, "That Mel has a sharp baseball eye. He agrees with me about our need for another reliever."

"Something will turn up," she said. "More toast?"

"No. I'm cutting down on starches. Something will turn up from *where*?"

"Who knows? Have faith, Mike. We've built our lives on it."

I suppose, if a man really loved this sport, winning or losing wouldn't matter, compared with the joy of being in it. This would be true—if we were not human beings.

Last year and the year before, I had hoped for better finishes, with no sensible reason to expect them, considering our personnel. They had given me the boys who could do it this year.

It is true that an inferior team that's up for any game can win it, and luck will always play its part. But in a 162-game season, luck has time to balance out and the cream is sure to rise. If I couldn't field a winner this year, I wouldn't deserve a new contract.

Heinie and I got to the stadium three hours before game time, sharing a cab. There were already hundreds of fans here. We would have a sellout.

"Will they love us in September as they do today?" Heinie asked.

I didn't answer, having none.

39

Baltimore would open with Jim Palmer, a 22-game winner last year, their ace of aces. We would go with Spack, who had won only 16, though he had finished the season with a lower era than Palmer. Leaky infields can falsify a pitcher's true earned run average.

It was warm for April, with hardly any breeze. Our golden boys, Ward and Cavanaugh, were co-hosting a press conference near the third base box seats.

"Let's get out of here," Heinie said. "I get my ears full of writer static all winter at the restaurant."

They probably weren't interested in a couple of old coots like us when they had quotable glamour pusses like those two.

The escape wasn't total; Rusty Jones was in the locker room, shooting the breeze with Bugs, our trainer, probably getting what they call a human interest story.

Rusty saw me and waved. I said, "Thanks for the plug."

"I stick with the truth," he answered. "It was all true."

They stick with what will sell papers, and occasionally it is the truth. "Right," I said.

The sun grew warmer and the stadium fuller. I went over the Baltimore roster with Luther Locust, our starting catcher. Luther had been in three All-Star games. That was quite a few years back, but physical condition was Luther's main religion, despite his name. And he had all he would ever need upstairs.

Due to the luck of rotation, we had faced Palmer only three times last season. He had beaten us all three times— Spack once, Jess Lepert twice. Our infield had been a bigger help to Palmer than to us in those games.

Myrna and Red Murphy's wife, Sheila, were in their box seats now, above the Titan dugout, starting their third season in the majors. They waved.

40

I tipped my cap to them and went over to watch Heinie giving a bunting lesson to Perry Washington. Perry, like his brother Willie, was quick and strong and agile. Unlike his brother, Perry spent more time arguing for black equality than proving it. Willie had nothing to prove; the whitest man on the club would have to admit Willie was not equal, he was superior.

Heinie had finally motivated Perry, working on what the shrinks call sibling rivalry. The lad had really put out this spring.

Heinie finished his lesson and Perry went to play catch with his brother.

"Lot of ballplayer behind that big mouth," Heinie commented. "I'm glad Myrna talked you into keeping him."

"Women are sentimental," I explained. "Work with Paige next. He's been crowding the plate too much and missing inside pitches."

"Right, boss. I'm hopeful, Mike."

"It's spring," I said.

Because I am by nature skeptical, Myrna and Mary claim I am a negative thinker. The way I see it, if you expect the worst, you will never be disappointed and often pleasantly surprised. To me, that is the acme of positive thinking.

And then it was time, the batting cards exchanged, the Anthem played. From behind the plate, Frosty Feldman, the League's senior umpire, called, "Play ball!" The first step on the long, rocky road had started.

My country bumpkin from Columbia U, Elmer Everett Spack, faced three men from last year's Divisional Championship winners and set them down in order.

In our half, Valdez steered a single past third, Oliver sacrificed him to second, Davis fouled out, and Paige struck out. This was not shaping up as any 17 to 16 slugfest.

41

The stadium was jammed, but quiet. The pitchers' dominance continued. It was bad boob tube baseball, but good aficionado baseball, tight and excellent, one hit, no runs, no errors through five innings.

In the sixth, Williams hit one out for them. Locust returned the favor in our half of the inning. Williams had hit .237 for the Orioles last year, but delivered 22 homers. Locust had hit .219 and delivered 17. With pitchers as sharp as Spack and Palmer, always around the plate, home runs can happen. It was 1 to 1, opening the seventh.

Spack had been throwing hard and the season was young. He seemed to tire in the inning, walking Robinson. Red went out to get his story. Red came back satisfied. If Red was, I was; we stayed with him. He finished the inning without damage, giving up a hit but no runs.

In our half, Joe Valdez came through with his second hit of the game, our third. Oliver went up, watching Heinie. Heinie relayed the signal from me—hit away. I had this hunch the pitchers' battle was about to end.

Chris hit away, all the way to left field, bouncing one off the fence, a standup double, sending Valdez to third.

Any long out now would put us in front, but my hunch remained strong. Kermit Davis was due up, still unhappy about not playing defense. He was in a mood to be fooled by cute pitching. Palmer might not be in a mood to play it cute—two up, two hits.

Kermit should hit to right, but he wasn't that clever a batter. Power was his sword. Go with the pitch, he was told.

Palmer steamed one, right over the heart of the plate. Kermit hit it, right into the center of the parking lot. Titans 4, Orioles 1, nobody out, last half of the seventh.

Watt came in and finessed them out of it without further

damage, one hit, no runs. We had a three-run edge and two innings to get through.

With last year's infield and bullpen, it would have been nervous-time in Titan Stadium. This year, I should have felt more comfortable. My nerves were not that healthy.

Spack took us through the eighth with a hit and a walk, no score. We got three long fly-ball outs against Watt. They would send the muscle up in the ninth—Coggins, Davis, and Baylor. I reached into my hip pocket, forgetting I hadn't brought my antacid tablets.

Your stomach shouldn't rumble, maybe, when you have a three-run lead in the ninth. It does if you have a memory.

Coggins grounded into an easy out—that wasn't. Ward threw wide to Oliver, pulling him off the bag. One on, no-body out. Spack smiled at Ward, trying to comfort the kid. A gentleman, that Spack, gentle and manly.

Davis grounded out to Heilbraun, Coggins taking second. And then Baylor came up and really creamed one, a low liner toward left field, rising all the way, sure to make the fence.

But Ward went sky-high to nail it—and there was Coggins, halfway to third. Back to Valdez for the double play.

Our ball game, 4 to 1. Playboy Algernon Ward had saved himself another sermon with that catch.

5

Starting pitchers do not often go nine innings these days, and certainly not in the first game of the season, when the money arm is still heavy with winter rust. Spack's performance had my stomach settled before I got home.

And at home, the smell of flavorful Irish stew filled the apartment. What finer feast for a settled stomach?

"Great game," Myrna said.

"Reassuring," I admitted. "I always feel safer when I don't have to go to the bullpen." I sat in the breakfast nook, where I could watch her work.

"Mary and Harvey are coming in for the Sunday game," she told me. "Leave their tickets with mine at the box office."

"Ha-ha!" I said. "You don't fool me. They are not coming in just for the game. They are coming in for our thirty-third wedding anniversary."

"Yes. Any regrets, Mike?"

"Very few. Only one, recently."

44

She turned from the sink to look at me.

"Last night," I explained, "when Mel and I were discussing our need for a short reliever, I saw a flicker in your eye. Something must have flashed in that file cabinet memory of yours. Who, Myrna?"

She shook her head. "You saw what wasn't there. I don't even remember the discussion. I'm sure you're not asking me to interfere in your business."

"Our agreement had an escape clause. *Publicly* interfering is not *privately* remembering."

"You saw what wasn't there," she repeated. "Wash up. The stew is almost ready."

The subservient hausfrau. . . . She wasn't fooling me. With her M.A. from NYU, with her IQ of 147, she wasn't fooling me. She would find a way to tell me, eventually, and still keep my age-eroded confidence alive.

At dinner, she said, "For your information, our anniversary is Monday. But Harvey has night appointments on Monday. That's why we're celebrating a day early."

Cavanaugh or Every, that was the decision I had labored over for the second game. I had decided, but not announced it to the press. I would go with Cavanaugh. To give the devil his due, he had sweated six years of alcohol out of his system under the Florida sun. He was as ready as he would ever be likely to be.

Nine years ago, it would have been an almost automatic win. He had won seventeen games in a row his second year with the Cardinals. Now? We would see, tomorrow.

That eminent birdbrain and noted non-thinker, Bart Witherspoon, was quoted in *The Times* sports pages next morning as prophesying the Orioles would breeze to the division crown, and were at least an even chance to take it all.

As for the Titans, he magnanimously conceded they might

45

climb to as high as third place this year—if they strengthened their bullpen. As for starters, he pointed out, they couldn't pitch Spack every day, could they?

Cy Elliott, the Oriole skipper, phoned before I left the house a couple of hours later. "I want to apologize for Bart's big mouth," he told me. "He has been reprimanded."

"No apology necessary, Cy. I owe you one, for cheating you on the deal."

"Heilbraun should help you and Witherspoon us. The way I see it, you boys have a much better than average chance to climb to second in the division this year."

"Thanks for calling, Cy." I hung up.

Cy was a Mormon. He would learn, in time, that Bart wasn't too crazy about them, either. A man who had been traded as often as Bart needed a lot of people to dislike.

The weather had changed overnight. It was overcast and gloomy, with a few drops of rain now and then. The forecast called for light rain by early afternoon. Rainouts lead to doubleheaders and doubleheaders are not for clubs with thin pitching staffs.

I used to say a small prayer, occasionallly, when I needed a win bad. But Mary found out about it and really scalded me. You do not ask The Lord for trivial things, she had explained, or any unfair advantage. That is a sacrilege.

Calling baseball a trivial thing is also a sacrilege, in my book, but I had promised her and I keep my promises.

Jimmy was already there, and in his uniform, when I got to the stadium. I didn't like his looks. He looked hung over to me, tight and shaky.

"Check him out," I told Red. "I have a feeling he may have resigned from AA last night."

Red shook his head. "I've already asked Ward. Jimmy was in bed at nine o'clock."

46

Ward stayed at Jimmy's apartment when they were in New York. I said, "Maybe he's got a cold or something. Have Bugs take his temperature. Or maybe Ward had a wild party and kept Cavanaugh from sleeping."

Red looked at me and sadly shook his head once more. "Mike, Mike, Mike! The man is pitching his first major league game in five years. Will you try to put yourself in his shoes?"

"They wouldn't fit," I said. "Okay, we'll stay with him until he falls apart."

Red said stiffly, "You hang onto your grudges almost as long as your money. It is my personal opinion we have us an *ace*!"

Red talks back to me as much as Heinie does, both being solvent. But if I only stuck with people who didn't talk back, I would have been divorced years ago. Difference of opinion is healthy, so long as everybody knows who's boss.

A drizzly day, a shaky pitcher. Doomsville, you're thinking. You'd be wrong. The kid put himself out on a limb often through three nervous innings—and crawled back safely each time, giving up four walks, three hits, but no runs. I should have remembered that, despite his many faults, the kid was still Irish.

The drizzle turned into a light rain in the fourth and the Baltimore bench started making remarks about endangering the lives of their delicate athletes, about umpires too dumb to come in out of the rain.

They were warned, but they kept muttering. They saw the way Cavanaugh was going, and realized one more half-inning would make it an official game. We were leading, 3 to 0, at the time.

The rain went away and the muttering stopped. Cavanaugh went seven and a third innings before they got to him, scoring with one man out in the eighth. Balding came in, and that was the end of that.

The ace of last year's Green Bay Pirates pitching staff was now 1 for 0 in the big time.

I should have gone with Every next day, but decided on Jess, knowing his spring weakness, playing a bad hunch. They got to him early and we never caught up. Their ball game, 7 to 2.

I must have looked extra sour, walking to the locker room. Clem Pelt said, "Can't win 'em all, Mike."

Clem is a competent coach, but not exactly an original thinker. I said, "Jess gave up three runs. Our bullpen gave up the other four. That is why I am not overwhelmed with joy."

We would host a two-game weekend series with Boston, then Monday off, followed by our first road trip. We were tied with two other clubs in the division for first place at .667. Only 159 games to go before the playoffs.

Boston had finished second in the division last year, beating us 14 times and losing only 4. They were good, but not that good. We had donated at least three of them with crucial errors.

Every started us off right against them this season, pitching a brainy game against Lee on Saturday afternoon, beating them, 4 to 2, with help from Balding. Detroit was the only club tied with us for the lead on Saturday night.

Sunday was something else, Spack against Tiant, a classic—if you had a lot of time to kill. They went through eight innings with identical stats, no runs, two hits, one walk each. Fisk put them ahead in the ninth with his first homer of the year. Chris Oliver's leg double and Paige's long single brought us back to even in our half.

Spack had gone a full nine innings in the season opener; he

had another nine behind him today. We watched him closely in the tenth.

He got past the lead-off man, striking him out on a 3-and-2 count. But then Heilbraun fumbled a trickler down the line and Aparicio walked. I sent in Vance Miller.

Balding had worked enough innings this week; Vance was the second best I had. He had been erratic in Florida, on again, off again. He was on, today. He pitched us out of the inning without damage, walking the first batter, and then serving up a perfect double-play ball.

It was still 1 to 1 in the twelfth when Vance weakened. He had two on and two out when Ritter came in to pinch hit. I had not counted on him; he was supposed to be injured.

Ritter *eats* right-handers, and usually *feasts* on Vance Miller. We would have our power coming up in the last half of the inning. I sent in Leeds to face Ritter.

Two pitches later, the score was 4 to 1. Our power coming up was not likely to be powerful enough. It hadn't been all afternoon. Bolin was on the mound for them by this time and going strong.

I will say this for my power boys, they tried. Davis walked, Paige singled, and Willie Washington brought them both home with a triple that missed being a homer by inches. With the tying run on third, and nobody out, I expected Cy to go to his bullpen.

He stuck with Bolin and he guessed right. Heilbraun popped out, Perry fouled out, and Ward struck out. Their ball game, 4 to 3.

It was a hard game to lose. There would be others.

Most of the boys were dressed, all of them had showered. Leeds sat in front of his locker, still in uniform. I went over.

"It happens, George," I said. "Don't dwell on it. It happens to all of us."

49

He looked up. He wasn't exactly crying, but his eyes were wet. "It happens to me too often," he said. "I love this game, skipper, but I don't think I belong up here—not yet."

"If you love the game, this is the only place to be. You have the potential, George. There's no way you could have come this high without it. You just keep doing the best you can and let us decide whether you belong up here."

"Those are the kids that get to me," I told Red later. "They eat, think, and sleep baseball and are always just one half-step short."

Red nodded. "The bushes are loaded with 'em. Well, I'll see you in a couple of hours." He gulped, and said quickly, "I mean tomorrow, of course."

Oh, sure he did. We were not going to have an anniversary dinner with Mary and Harve. We were going to have a surprise party, full of old friends. That Myrna. . . .

It wasn't that big a party, just Harve and Mary, Clem and Alice Pelt, Heinie and Rose, Red and Sheila. That was it—until about five minutes before we were due to sit down for dinner.

And then Myrna went to the door. And who should walk in but Tony Bernardi!

He had been my bat boy at Newark. He had gone with Mary all through high school. If God had seen fit to bestow a son on me, I'm sure He would have had the grace to send me Tony Bernardi. I would have had to be an Italian, of course, to complete the deal, but He could arrange that.

Tony's real papa owned seven or eight manufacturing plants in Jersey and a few banks, but there wasn't enough money in the world to spoil this kid.

He came over to hug me, in his Latin way. "Uncle Mike," he said, "my Celtic paisan!"

50

"What are you doing here," I asked, "with your club in Detroit?"

"I'm not with Cleveland anymore," he said. "I'm working at one of my father's banks in Camden."

That didn't make sense, but I didn't have time to find out why. Mary came over, squealing with delight, and dragged him away to introduce him to Harve.

Myrna still stood there, looking sly. "I ran into him at Selvedge's in January," she explained, "when I went to that drape sale. He told me then about all the shenanigans his father was planning to get Cleveland to release him. His father thought he should know more about the family business. He's the oldest son."

"Get him released? How could he? There's no way!"

"He could if he bought the club, couldn't he?"

"Salvatore Bernardi," I said patiently, "does not own the Cleveland Indians."

"I am not a financial tycoon, Mike. Finance bores me. I don't want to understand the mechanics of it. He must have bought enough stock to threaten them with a proxy fight, because that's what he did. And last week sold the stock at a nice profit, according to Tony." She sighed. "I wanted him to be here, at our anniversary, and so did Mary. He's almost family, Mike!"

"You are a sweet and intelligent woman," I said, "who has gone underground. I have this strange feeling that you have also learned Tony is now bored with the banking business."

"It's time to eat," she said.

6

Nineteen colleges had offered Tony an athletic scholarship when he graduated from high school. He needed the financial help almost as much as David Rockefeller. And if there is one thing an old country Italian desires for his American son, it is to see him in a classy school. So Tony had gone to Harvard—and pitched them to three Ivy League championships.

I'd tried to sell Mel King on him while I was still at Newark. It was one time when Mel and I didn't see eye to eye, his error. Tony had a minor asthmatic problem; more than five innings against big league bats was too long for him, right from his first year. But I had seen him once, against Mel's Titans, with the bases loaded, strike out the heart of the order on nine pitches, no bat touching the ball.

I phoned Deke Briggs, the club secretary, Monday morning. "Can you get in touch with Wiltern?" I asked.

"If I have to. Is it important?"

"It could be more important than improving his tan on the

Mediterranean beaches. I think we can sign Tony Bernardi.''

"You must be kidding, Mike! Old man Bernardi almost destroyed Cleveland, getting the lad into the family business.''

"There is another son, now graduated from Yale, just aching to take over.''

"Where'd you hear all this?''

"In the drapery department at Selvedge's. I haven't the time for long explanations. Our plane for Detroit leaves in an hour. Can you get to Wiltern today?''

"If necessary. Is Bernardi in shape?''

"You handle the paper, Deke. I'll handle the ivory. Each to his own.''

"Okay! You don't have to get snotty! I won't need Mr. Wiltern on this. I'm authorized.''

He was authorized—to empty the ash trays. "Phone me in Detroit,'' I said, "if it's the next three days. Then we move to Milwaukee.''

"I am fully cognizant of the club schedule,'' he said, and hung up.

Deke could have made it on the playing field—if some club had needed a slow outfielder with a hole in his glove who batted .183. He had made it into the front office the hard way, by marrying our owner's homeliest cousin.

Detroit would send Coleman against us, a 23-game winner last year. We would go with Cavanaugh. It was gloomy in New York when we took off; it was raining in Detroit when we landed. The Detroit weatherman predicted clear skies for tomorrow. He could be wrong.

If it rained, Golden Jimmy would have his second wet outing in two starts. Should I go with Every if it rained? He'd had three days' rest.

53

I asked Red.

He smiled. "Softening of the heart? What do *you* care if *he* gets pneumonia?"

"He's one of us, isn't he? Was there ever a time I was unfair to one of our players?"

"Jimmy's healthy," he said, "and he's ready."

He was healthy, he was ready, and it didn't rain. Cleveland had just left here, losing two out of three. We couldn't do worse, after the opener. Cavanaugh beat Coleman, Miller pitching the last two innings. Our bats beat Lolich, 8 to 7, in the second game, though Every got credit for the win. Jess Lepert went four innings in the final game and gave up three runs. Balding came in and gave up one more. Leeds finished the game, giving up none. Their ball game, 4 to 2.

Deke Briggs didn't phone me in Detroit, so I phoned him from Milwaukee, collect, Friday morning. "What goes on?" I asked.

"Tony's agreeable," he told me. "Cleveland's giving us trouble, threatening to go to the Commissioner."

"Why? They released him, didn't they?"

"To go into business, not to another club."

I told him what he could tell Cleveland, unprintable.

"That isn't the way things are done," he protested.

"That is the way things are done in the real world, busher. Have Tony explain it to his papa. Salvatore will straighten it out. I'm sure Cleveland doesn't want to be bought and converted into a girls' volleyball team."

"I may have been a busher, Mike, though I resent your reminding me. You take care of the ivory. I'll take care of the paper." He hung up.

I phoned Tony at the Camden bank. I told him, "We have an innocent child in the front office trying to handle a man's

54

job. Explain it to your father, but don't inform Briggs.''

"I already have," he said. "It should be all cleared up before you get back to New York. May I have my old Cleveland number?''

"If it's available. If it isn't, I'll make it available. You're in shape, aren't you?''

"Right. I've been working out with the Camden Comets. I have an unshakable feeling I am finally going to pitch in a World Series.''

"Your intincts are sound. Hang in there, son.''

A pitcher from the Camden Comets and another from the Green Bay Pirates, does that look like a Series-bound club? A clever manager, with good help from his staff, might manage it.

When I told Red about the call, he said, "We'll have to make room for him. Should we send Leeds back to Oil City?''

I thought of the kid, sitting in front of his locker, his eyes wet. I said, "Not yet. There must be one of those alleged utility infielders we can drop. Leeds looked sharper yesterday than he has all spring.''

Milwaukee was the only club that had finished behind us in the division last year. The citizens of Beer Town had enjoyed their glory days in that other league, with Mr. Aaron's Braves, assisted by Mathews and Spahn. The Brewers were a few years away from that level of excellence.

They didn't lay down and die. Colborn fought Spack through every inning before losing, 2 to 1. They jumped on Cavanaugh in the first inning of Saturday's game. Balding went in, followed by Miller, relieved by Dorn, relieved by Leeds. The loss was Dorn's, 8 to 6. I should have brought in Leeds earlier.

Every won us the rubber game, with help from the hot bats of the Washington brothers, three hits each, and relief help in the eighth from Balding.

We had faced four clubs, won three series, split the other. We had 7 wins and 4 losses. Last year at this time, we had lost 8 and won 3. Last year is not this year. Yesterday is not today or tomorrow. We may have come home a little smug.

Some of the weaker Western Division clubs were coming to town. We figured to fatten up on them.

Tony reported Tuesday, but he wouldn't be usable for a couple of weeks. Pitching part-time for the Camden Comets is not big league conditioning.

Spack had come home with three wins and no losses, his best spring record ever. He left town with the same number of wins—and two losses. Ryan of the Angels beat him 2 to 1. Bahnsen of the White Sox beat him 3 to 2. He didn't pitch against the Rangers. The teams we faced in that stand had comprised the bottom half of the Western Division last year. They won 5 from us and lost only 3.

It wasn't the pitching, either starters or relievers, and our fielding was stable. For the first time in my memory, a whole club went into a hitting slump as a community effort. It happens to individual players every year, and can hurt you. A mass slump can *destroy* you.

Heinie worked them overtime at batting practice, but a plague like that is not physical, it is mental. A locker room pep talk wouldn't do any good; their main fault was that they were already trying too hard, pressing.

Leeds was improving, and gaining confidence. Despite his last two losses, Spack had an era of 2.14. Balding was everything we had hoped for and Tony would be. Every was sound, Jess getting stronger. Cavanaugh had been bombed

56

twice; I forced myself to keep an open mind about him.

We had the pitching. Now, if only somebody would find the ball with his bat.

We were still over .500, with 10 wins and 9 losses, when we started on our first western road trip. We had hosted the losers on the home stand. We would be visiting the winners on the road, Minnesota and Kansas City.

I know, I know, you play each one as it comes up; today is here, tomorrow may never come. It is the only way to go. Unfortunately, I am not that kind of man, having spent most of my life scanning the clouds on the horizon.

Cavanaugh would open against Kansas City. As I stood near the far end of the dugout, watching him warm up Tuesday night, I must have been looking unhappy.

Because Red asked, "Sour stomach again, Mike?"

"That last home stand was not exactly an aid to good digestion. And facing the Royals with a refugee from the Green Bay Pirates is not likely to change it."

"We won three of the eight," he pointed out. "One-third of our wins was Cavanaugh's."

He had beaten Texas, 5 to 4. Four of our runs were unearned, contributed by Texas fielding. Red knew that, so I didn't remind him. And Cavanaugh had been relieved by Miller in the sixth, which he also knew, and I didn't mention. I was getting weary of arguing with Cavanaugh fans.

He patted my shoulder. "Cheer up, Mike. In a couple of days, the ace of the Camden Comets should be ready."

Maybe it was going to early mass that did it for Cavanaugh. Or maybe the boys had packed their hitting clothes by mistake when they left New York. They knocked out two pitchers and shook up the third in our half of the first inning.

Golden Jimmy took the mound for the last half of the inning with seven runs already in the bank. He managed to load the bases immediately, the first three up, and I almost yanked him.

But then Carl Heilbraun, playing deep, pulled off the first unassisted triple play I had ever seen in my long life, spearing what should have been a cinch double off the bat of Schaal, stepping on third, tagging the runner racing down from second before he could turn around. Even the Royal fans gave him a standing ovation as he trotted in.

"A heady, steady Kraut," Heinie said, "just like I told you in January."

"I figured a triple play was about due," I explained. "That's why I didn't pull Cavanaugh."

Cavanaugh gave up four runs in five and two-thirds innings. We were leading 8 to 4, with two out and runners on second and third, when I sent in Balding.

He got us the third out on an infield pop. But it was cold, this May night in Kansas City, and Balding was not young. He stiffened in the eighth. Leeds finished the game for us, getting further from Oil City with every outing.

"Two wins in a row for Cavanaugh," Red commented.

"If we can continue to get him seven runs in the first inning," I admitted, "he should work out okay."

We would face Splittorff tomorrow night. He had won 20 games for them last year, but his earned run average hadn't been that great. If our bats stayed hot. . . .

Our bats were as hot as the temperature, 47 degrees at game time, and getting colder. Cal Every is from Helena, Montana, so 47-degree weather didn't feel cold to him. He took us through five innings with only one run allowed. We had come up with none.

In the sixth, Splittorff got careless with Luther, way down there at the bottom of the order, and tried to blow him down with fastballs. Luther eased one into the bleachers and we were tied.

It stayed tied through the seventh and the eighth and our half of the ninth. Then, with two out in their half, Mayberry came up and knocked one out.

Cal Every had allowed only four hits and lost a ball game. If he'd had Cavanaugh's luck. . . .

Unless it warmed up, Jess Lepert would be a bad choice for tomorrow night. I asked Red what he thought.

"We could start Dorn," he suggested. "He started a couple for us early last year, remember?"

"He's only good for about four innings," I said.

"Then Leeds? And Tony's almost ready."

"We'll try it," I decided.

The weather stayed cold; we started with Lem Dorn. He is a slow and deliberate worker, his greatest asset his ability to make batters impatient. By the time Lem gets ready to throw, they are so relieved to see the ball finally coming their way they are inclined to swing at bad pitches, of which Lem has a wide assortment.

He was warned by the umpire three times, but continued to study the empty bases as though they were full, to reposition his outfielders, to shake off pitches he knew he was going to throw.

The Royals started to jockey him from the bench, but Lem doesn't wear his hearing aid on the field. He was warned for the last time in the third inning about Official Rule 8-4, the twenty-second rule, honored only by its infrequency of application.

He managed to deliver in nineteen and nine-tenths seconds after that, but Luther took his time returning the ball to him, examining it often for possible defects.

It was a farce of a game. Sid Gomer, the plate umpire,

came over to warn me, "I could give it to the Royals by default. I don't enjoy watching clowns in baseball suits on a night as cold as this."

"There may be such a default rule in your mind, Sid," I said. "We both know it has never been dignified by print. I'll speak to Dorn."

We were leading, 1 to 0, at the time, on a scratch single by Valdez and a triple by Kermit Davis. Red went out to tell Dorn to speed it up.

Which Lem did—which Piniella knocked over the fence—1 to 1.

"We can't beat ten men!" Heinie shouted.

Sid turned to glare at Heinie, but said nothing. Sid, too, eats at Heinie's in the off season.

It kept getting colder and the fans noisier, the ones who hadn't already left for their warm hearths.

In the fifth, with one on and one out, I sent in Bernardi. It was cold enough by now to clearly see the smoke trailing his blazers. The change in velocity sent two Royals down on seven pitches. Both batters were completing their swings as Luther was returning the ball to the mound.

"He's faster than Feller ever was," Red said. "But speed's about all he's got, isn't it, Mike?"

"Plus confidence," I added, "the natural confidence which comes from being born rich, as F. Scott Fitzgerald once explained."

"Fitzgerald? Doesn't he write for the *Post-Dispatch*?"

"He wrote for the literate public," I informed him. "Ask Sheila."

In the eighth, the Royals began to guess right on Tony's speed. There were two on and two out when I sent Leeds in. He got us the third out with slow teasers, annoying the few fans left in the park.

60

Heilbraun, Perry Washington, and Ward combined to get us the go ahead run in the ninth. Leeds finished for his first win—and our first series win in too long a time.

Going from Kansas City to Minnesota, you would have to assume it would be colder in Minnesota. Going from anywhere except Siberia, you would have to assume that.

But the sun was out in Bloomington and the Twins management had patriotically decided to do their bit during the current energy crisis. We would play three day games.

It was a noble gesture, though not to our advantage. It had been a long, mean night in Kansas City, and then our plane had been delayed by a bomb threat, undoubtedly phoned in by some disgruntled Royals fan.

Spack was tired. He showed it in the first inning, walking the first batter, serving up a long single to the second. Any other pitcher, I might have pulled. I had a lot of faith in this man; I decided to let him face one more batter before going out. The batter was Oliva. It was 3 to 0, Twins leading.

I sent in Miller, who gave up another before settling down. A 4–0 lead is too high a mountain for a tired team to climb. We managed to pick up a couple in the eighth. Their game, 6 to 2.

Our bats were a few degrees hotter than they had been on the home stand. Tomorrow, if the Cavanaugh luck held, we should have a chance to even the series.

The Cavanaugh luck held. He gave up seven hits and two walks in the first five innings. Our infield supported him with two double plays. Our outfield (in the person of Otis Paige) came through with a spectacular throw from center field to nip Carew at the plate.

We were leading 2–0, when Hisle opened their half of the sixth with a double. I looked at Red. Red shrugged.

I forget who batted next, but he really tagged one—straight

61

at Valdez, who tossed to Ward, covering, catching Hisle off the bag. From one on and nobody out, we had gone to none on and two out. The fabled luck of the Irish is unevenly distributed.

The law of averages began to catch up with him in the eighth, two on, two out. My foster son went in, carrying his sword. Luther put a sponge inside his glove.

Flash, streak, ball of fire—2–0, end of the eighth.

We came up with nothing in the ninth. They came up with nothing through the first two batters. Then Terrell walked up and hit one out, his first of the year. Last year, through 438 times at bat in 124 games, he had amassed a grand total of one home run. With Tony's speed, a high bunt will carry out.

I looked at Red. Red shrugged. I don't get too much help at critical moments, though any numbskull fan can tell you what you did wrong, after the game.

Tony looked my way and smiled. I went out there and asked him, "Everything okay?"

"Everything is fine and dandy, Uncle Mike. Two to zip, or two to one, what's the difference? They're both wins."

"Fire away," I said, and went back to the dugout.

Brye walked to the plate and creamed one, sending Paige up against the wall in center field for the catch. We had evened the series.

Tomorrow will be warm, stated the weatherman. Tomorrow, Every will be ready, I decided, after a laborious, penetrating analysis.

He was ready—and they were waiting. I took him out, after the first four runs, and sent in Balding. He gave up three more on a homer to Oliva, his second in two days, his second time up in the inning.

A 7–0 score in the first inning? That is not baseball. Football, maybe, or some of the other brutal sports. What man can prepare for the absurd?

It was all they got, but it was enough, 7 to 3.

As we walked to the locker room, Clem said to Red, "Five hundred on the road against top Western contenders? I'll settle for that, any time."

"Right!" Red said.

Blithe spirits, unburdened by the weight of management.

7

We moved erratically through May, lions one day, lambs the next, no consistency, good or bad, a club going along like a drifting log on a lazy river.

We stayed close to .500, thanks to the matching ennui of our divisional competitors. Nobody seemed to want the flag. Baltimore and Boston traded first place every other day. In the middle of June, Detroit, in fourth place, was only a game and a half behind Baltimore, in first.

It was my personal opinion we had the best balanced club in either division and should have led all the way. There is bound to be bias in personal opinions, but Heinie agreed with me.

"It might be time for a few well chosen words," he suggested, "delivered with your usual acid touch."

"I was thinking of something in a more paternal and benevolent vein," I answered.

"Who'd write it for you?"

I stared at him.

"I see your point," he said. "The boys aren't really loafing. A gentle urging, maybe?"

"Something along that line."

What I told them was, "We have been drifting. Nobody has been loafing, but not all of us are putting out the extra ten percent that makes a champion. I think we are as strong as any club in either division. We might be the best in the whole country; I haven't been keeping track of that other league. We are playing as well as any of them, but one of the clubs has to start a drive soon. I would like it to be us."

That was the middle of June, as I said. It took some time for the full import of my words to filter through. We didn't get our drive underway until the first week in August. We swept three from Boston, won two out of three from Baltimore. For the first time that season, we were in unshared first place.

As a manager, I had been in first place often in Newark. It was a novel experience for me in New York. My natural good nature might have soured some under the tension.

"We're sound and we're moving," Myrna said one night. "Relax, Mike."

It was the first time she had initiated a baseball discussion in months. I stared at her, perplexed.

"You're mumbling in your sleep," she explained. "You're even more sarcastic than usual. I can take it, but if you're the same way around the boys, it could lead to club dissension."

"It could lead to club unity, too," I pointed out. "They could all hate me together."

"That's a theory too sophisticated for me," she said.

"Myrna, there are five clubs in the division who hate to see us up there at the top. They are all making plans to reverse the trend. That's bound to make a manager nervous."

"Hot on the inside, cool on the outside, Mike. How many times have you told me that's the only way to go?"

"I was younger then."

"You were fifty-seven, the last time you told me. And this is the last time I will break my promise about not interfering in your business."

I asked Heinie at batting practice next day, "Am I more ornery than usual lately?"

"We all are," he answered. "You have always been our leader in that department, but I haven't noticed much change."

"Myrna thinks I am."

"Well, she sees more of you than I do, now that you've stopped playing gin. Mike, we're what we are, and too old to change."

And maybe too old to manage kids? I wondered. The Iowa Sage? Never!

In the middle of August, we were still in front by two full games. Cavanaugh's luck was holding, Spack was his invincible self, and Jess Lepert's blood had been warmed by the summer sun. I rotated him out when we visited California, where it is always around 23 degrees below zero for night games, spring, summer, and fall.

Ward had finally begun to understand big league pitching; I moved him up to sixth in the order, dropping Heilbraun to eighth. Both Washington brothers were hitting solidly, and Valdez knew more ways to get on base than most batters realize there are. Kermit Davis had lost his sulks, basking in the glory of leading the division among designated hitters.

There were clouds on the horizon, though they were small. Both Baltimore and Boston were fattening up on the tail-enders, while we were meeting the cream of the west, due to their luck in scheduling. In September, when all play was confined to each division, we would bring them back to reality.

On September 5th, we were leading Boston by a full game, Baltimore by half a game. I assembled my happy warriors for a word of caution.

"We are the finest baseball team," I told them, "within the continental limits of North America, which means the world. But excellence is not always enough. A baseball can take many strange bounces and lesser teams quite often play over their heads. The months behind will mean nothing if we do not continue to perform well in this decisive period. For the next thirty days, I expect you to spurn all the worldly diversions that can cheat us out of a champion's just reward, both spiritual and financial. This month, I want you to live and think baseball for twenty-four hours in each of the thirty days."

They filed out quietly.

"Well put?" I asked Heinie.

He looked doubtful. "I don't know, Mike. It might have been a little on the negative side."

Heinie was not a reader; he had been the wrong man to ask about words.

We were facing Detroit that day, while Boston faced Cleveland and Baltimore was idle.

Lucky Jimmy would face Lolich, a man he had already beaten twice this season. Detroit had sagged in the early part of August, come on stronger the last half of the month. Lolich was not the star he had been, but there were still twenty-three other clubs that would be happy to have him.

Jimmy stumbled through five batters and came out unscathed.

"That man's luck is unbelievable," I told Red.

Red shook his head. "He is no longer eighteen, Mike, upstairs or downstairs. He knows which pitches are crucial and he saves his diminishing strength for them."

"At his age," I said, "I could shoulder three hundred pounds."

"At his age," Red said, "the strongest drink you had ever consumed was cinnamon tea."

I went over to stand at the other end of the dugout.

It went along like that, Jimmy's luck versus Lolich's skill. Then Ward let a hot grounder streak through between his legs. Before the ball could be run down, Cash was on second. Single or double, it wouldn't have mattered. Horton came up and hit one out. It was 2–0, Tigers on top.

Ward opened the sixth and partially redeemed himself, lining a triple that bounced around in the left-field corner. Perry brought him home with a long out to right field—2–1, end of the sixth.

Normally, I would have trusted my instincts and pulled Cavanaugh. But I had received so many contradictory opinions in the last twenty-four hours, my self-confidence had been eroded. I let him start the seventh.

Three runs later, I sent in Balding. He worked us out of the inning, but the damage had been done. Detroit had a four-run lead and Lolich on the mound. We nicked him for a run in the ninth, and had two runners on, when Strahler came in to save it for them.

Boston had beaten Cleveland. We were still in first place. So were Boston and Baltimore, all of us tied at .580.

I went back to my instincts next day, starting Jess instead of Every. Every had a slight cold; he could use an extra day's rest. It was a day game and it would be a hot day and Jess had always had good luck against Detroit.

As Heinie and I watched him warm up next afternoon, Heinie asked, "Were Jimmy and Tony the only boys Mary ever went with?"

"Of course not! She was a very popular girl! What kind of dumb question is that?"

"I was thinking about next year," he said. "Jess might be too old to help us by then. I thought Mary might know some other pitchers."

"Just stick with this year," I advised him, "and next year will take care of itself."

Jess turned out to be a good hunch, my first in the last three. He threw sliders at them and palm balls, what he laughingly referred to as his fastball, and even a few knucklers. There were cynical critics who claimed Jess also threw spitters, but the charge was patently false. Jess did not have enough juice left in him to waste on spit.

Young men do not like to be humiliated by older men. The more annoyed the batters became, the less chance they had of hitting the ball. Jess went through seven innings, allowing six hits and no runs. We had a 3 to 0 lead when he began to tire in the eighth.

I didn't wait. I sent in my millionaire fireballer. He gave up one hit through two innings, a homer to McAuliffe. Our game, 3 to 1.

Getting on the plane for Cleveland that night, we were a game ahead of Boston, who had lost, dead even with Baltimore, who had won.

We were winging our way toward a hostile crowd. The fans in Cleveland were still unhappy and suspicious about the Bernardi transfer, and they had let us know about it on every visit. I had kept Tony out of all the games there, leery of starting a riot.

Every still had a few sniffles, but his temperature was almost normal. He opened the series for us. His record against the Indians was as good as any on the staff. Cal is a man aware of his records; his confidence was strong. His fastball, however, was slow. He gave up three hits for a run in the first inning.

He threw the fastball sparingly after that and had their bats doing minimum damage through the fourth.

In the fifth, Tidrow got careless with Luther. Our bottom-of-the-order man tied it up with his thirteenth homer of the year.

The fans who were there were noisy, but a club in last place in September doesn't attract too many fans, even in Cleveland. They didn't bother Cal. He worked his way carefully, preserving the tie.

He gave up two very long, loud outs in the eighth, and I looked at Red.

"One more," Red suggested.

Brohammer was due up; I stuck with Cal. Brohammer popped to Oliver, ending the inning. Red and I had guessed right.

Oliver, Davis, and Paige got us a run in the ninth with two hits and a sacrifice bunt. We were three outs away from a win.

The long outs in the eighth had been a signal. When the Indians began to stir up dust in their half of the inning, Leeds went in.

Two on, only one out, a slim one-run lead; it could have been a bad time to test a rookie. He had earned the right to prove himself. Baseball is more than a printed won-lost account in a record book. It is a game played by humans accepting challenge.

It was a triumphant challenge for George Leeds. The first

batter he faced struck out, the second one grounded out.

"We were right about him," Red said. "I'm glad we didn't send him down this spring."

Red had suggested sending him down, the way I remembered it. I made no comment, only nodding.

Baltimore had lost, Boston had won. We were a full game in front of both of them.

Spack breezed the next night, allowing only three hits, a double, and two squib singles. He could have allowed more; we came up with six runs, every batter but Oliver getting at least one hit.

Balance, that's what warms a manager's heart in September. My stomach was evidently not in communication with my heart, staying queasy.

Cavanaugh's arrogance cost us the getaway game. He led all the way through the sixth, thanks to our bats. We had a 7–4 edge in the last half of the seventh when Cavanaugh faced Hendrick with two out and two on.

He must have known, as Every had in the opener, that his fastball had no zip. Luther didn't call for it, but Golden Jimmy threw it—and we had a tied ball game.

One thing a club doesn't need in a stretch drive is an extra inning game on getaway day. We went thirteen innings before Cleveland won it, 9 to 8.

In the locker room, I told Cavanaugh, "Next time, listen to Luther. He's been around these hitters a lot longer than you have."

He nodded.

"That was an expensive pitch you threw," I went on. "I have decided it will cost you a hundred dollars."

He said nothing. But Algernon Ward, dressing next to him, said, "That's not right, skipper. You can't fine a man for giving up a home run. The Commissioner would never stand still for it. He'd overrule you."

"I was talking to Cavanaugh," I said, "not to you. Have you some paper that shows you are his legal agent?"

He shook his head.

"Then keep your mouth shut," I said.

He glared at me and I stared back. He followed my advice, keeping his mouth shut.

Heinie had overseen and overheard it. "Dumb, Mike," he said.

"Maybe. All right, yes! Probably illegal, too. So, I'll rescind it."

"Right now," he suggested, "and include a few soft words. You were wrong and Ward was right. *Now,* Mike, before it gets out of hand. This is showdown month. We can't afford any friction."

"Not now," I said. "I am not in a mood for it now, nor for any discussion on the subject."

It had been dumb of me. Thirteen innings of a lost game in front of a jeering crowd watching a game that should have been won by us in nine might be an excuse for overreacting, but that is a luxury managers are not permitted. I would visit the boys in their room tomorrow and explain my rancor.

I called their room five times next day, but they weren't in. Maybe they just weren't answering their phone; I went over to their room and knocked. Nothing. We were in Milwaukee. I learned from Bugs, half an hour later, that they had gone out to the town's famous zoo. They were both animal lovers, plus the other.

I would get them to one side out at the park, I decided, and state my piece. Then Heinie had this idea that we should go to Mader's for some German cooking. By the time we got to the park, it was almost game time.

So call it a lapse, call it an error. I had overreacted. The way I see it, Ward did, too, later.

We took two out of three from Milwaukee and moved on to Baltimore. This was the team we had to beat, this one and Boston. Knocking off the also-rans helps the average; knocking off the contenders helps exactly twice as much.

We wouldn't have to worry about any bean balls from Witherspoon; he had been sent down to one of their farm clubs in August. All we had to worry about was gaining ground on last year's divisional champs.

The first two games were laughers, one for them, one for us. They pounded Jess and Dorn for eight runs in the first game, and won it. We supported Every with nine, and won the second.

The rubber game was more related to baseball, Spack versus Palmer. Winning or losing, that was a game to watch—unless you had a partisan interest in it and a nervous stomach.

Spack gave up two hits and no runs through five. Palmer gave up *no* hits and no runs. Both of their hits had been scratchy, six of Palmer's fifteen outs had been strikeouts.

He still had the no-hitter going through the seventh, and tension in the stadium was growing. There were undoubtedly fans in the park who had followed baseball all their lives and never seen a no-hitter. If this hadn't been September, I might have been rooting for Palmer myself.

When he went through the eighth with two infield outs and a strikeout, you could almost feel the weight of the tension from the stands pressing down on the field.

"Great pitcher," Heinie said.

"Two great pitchers," I said. "This will be a mean game for either of us to lose."

Palmer had two outs in our half of the ninth, and a strike

73

on Otis Paige, when the spell was broken. He hung a curve ball and Otis slammed it into the cheap seats. Titans 1, Orioles 0, middle of the ninth.

"Spack look tired to you?" I asked Red.

He shook his head. "But Palmer sure did, walking off. You know, I was rooting for him?"

"I almost was myself," I admitted. "But it is not the season for compassion."

"Not for eleven o'clock Catholics," Red said.

Spack held them. We had come into Baltimore and picked up a full game. We now led them by two.

8

I knew when I came home that night that something was bothering Myrna. At breakfast, next morning, I asked her what it was.

"I'd have to break my promise," she said.

"Break it."

"All right then, that item in Rusty Jones' column, was it the truth?"

"I don't read Rusty Jones on the road. What did he say?"

"He said you had fined Jimmy for giving up a home run and had a locker room run-in with Al Ward."

"It's more or less true." I told her the whole story, not sparing myself, including the five phone calls, the trip to their room, and the dinner at Mader's.

"Did you later explain this to them," she asked, "and publicly rescind the fine?"

I shook my head. "I explained nothing, due to the events I have described, and *privately* rescinded the fine."

"And you don't plan to explain it to them?"

"Not anymore. It's too late."

She said nothing, looking thoughtful.

"What are you thinking?" I asked.

"I'm thinking I should have doubled Sheila, yesterday afternoon, when she bid the grand slam. More coffee?"

We took the opener from Detroit, our left-handed lover boy pitching his strongest game of the season, giving up only three hits.

"Like him better now?" Heinie asked.

"I have a professional admiration for his performance. I am also an emotional man, cursed with a long memory."

He sighed and shook his head. "I'm glad I don't have *your* memory!"

"Your bad memory has served me well, Heinie. Otherwise, you would be able to remember which cards I discarded."

Detroit took the second game, splitting the series. They left town and Boston moved in.

I was back on the stomach tablets by this time and not talking too much, well aware of my talent for being misunderstood. Silence is not natural for me, making me even more edgy than usual.

That was a bad time for the hack from the *News* to write his so-called profile on Algernon Ward, including some of our rookie's opinions on the state of the world and the defects of a number of its citizens. One of the citizens evaluated was yours truly.

What he was quoted as saying about me was that, though nobody could question my minor league managerial success, it was possible I was too out of touch with the younger generation to succeed at my profession in today's changing world.

These were the words of a boy who had probably graduated in the bottom tenth of his class from Delinquent High School, in Mishap, Missouri, but the hack quoted them as though he had just interviewed Ralph Waldo Emerson.

I had the lad sent in before the Boston game, and smiled kindly at him when he entered.

He stood there, neither smiling nor looking scared.

"You are quite a man for opinions," I told him. "September is usually a bad month for them."

"The truth can never hurt anybody," he said.

"I suppose that statement is not much falser than any other generality. What I want to know is—what's your beef with me?"

He gave it a few seconds of thought, searching for the elusive truth, no doubt. Then, "Jimmy. Jimmy Cavanaugh. I admire him very, very much. He is a man walking a tightrope, a man on thin ice, a man with a problem he has to work every minute of every day to lick. The way you treat him, you could push him over the edge."

"I could also push him into the Hall of Fame. He's never pitched better than he has the last couple of weeks, since that night I overreacted in Cleveland. I'm sorry about that night and I admit it."

"You could have said that earlier."

"I could have. I didn't, for reasons I don't think I have to explain to a rookie. But I was wrong then, and because of that, I am going to go easy on you. I am going to fine you, for necessary disciplinary reasons, but it will be only a token fine, ten dollars."

"I won't pay it," he said evenly. "If you take it out of my pay, I'll sue."

I stared at him and he didn't look away. My stomach rumbled. I kept my voice low. "You will sit on the bench until you do. You could cost your teammates a World Series check, sitting on the bench.''

"I have to live by my principles," he said. "Is that all?"

"Until you come up with the ten dollars, that's all. Dismissed."

I played Art Stark at shortstop that night, batting him ninth in the order, moving the sixth, seventh, eighth, and ninth batters up a notch. Ward had been batting fifth, lately.

The only thing weaker than Art's glove was his bat. Kermit Davis was a bad second choice. He could hit and was hitting, but his brain was not up to Art's, his glove about equal. He was where he belonged, at designated hitter.

Well, it would be only a day or two. Algernon Ward had too much competitive instinct in him to miss the action for a mere ten dollars.

When I gave Heinie the batting card to take out, he studied it and frowned. "Ward sick?"

"Not that I know of. It's a disciplinary measure."

"Because of that dumb piece in the *News*?"

"Take the card out, Heinie. The umpire's waiting."

Boston would open with Tiant. He had given us trouble this year, and every year. Cunning Jess Lepert would face him. It was a warm night for September; Jess should be functioning well.

When he took the mound, he glanced over at shortstop, paused, and looked my way. *Adjust,* I tried to tell him through extrasensory perception. *Do not give right-handed batters anything they can pull.*

He nodded, as though he'd received the message.

I should not have relied on his sensitivity. The first man up pulled one right through Stark's legs, rolling it all the way to the outfield. Jess looked my way again, as though *I* had blown the grounder.

The runner had only reached first, running it routinely, assuming it would be an out. That saved us the run. Because, after the next batter fouled out, Cepeda came up and hit a single long enough to bring even a turtle home from second. With runners on first and third, my senior staffer reached into his arsenal of junk pitches and conned them out of further damage.

"If his arm was as strong as his brain," Red said, "we'd be in first place by ten games. Ward sick?"

I shook my head.

A few seconds of silence, and then, "I didn't know you read the *Daily News*."

I said nothing.

He sighed. "There goes the fun-filled trip to Bermuda I promised Sheila. We were counting on at least playoff money."

I had no comment.

Jess had his memory and his skill and we had luck, very few balls being hit to shortstop. For the second time in two years, we beat Tiant. Boston was another foot deeper in the swamp, and sinking.

Spack looked unbeatable the next night, playing catch with Luther through seven innings. In the eighth, Stark blew one and Elmer let it ruffle him, rare for him. He walked Smith. We had a two-run lead but I didn't like Elmer's attitude. I sent in Bernardi.

Courage is grace under pressure, as Mr. Hemingway said. Tony went through the next six batters as though they were unworthy pretenders to the throne, challenging each, sending each back, chastened, to his home fort.

We had taken two in a row from Boston without the active participation of Algernon Ward.

Cavanaugh pitched the third game, walking a tightrope

over the thin ice with his usual abandon, bestowing hits and walks as though each batter he faced was on welfare.

"He needs Ward out there," Red observed. "It's a thing with him."

I said nothing, sending in Balding.

They got no runs off him, but it was too late. Their game, 4 to 3.

Deke Briggs phoned me two hours before we were due to take off for Detroit. "What's with Ward?" he asked.

"I don't know. Has he asked for a raise? I don't understand the question."

"Don't be evasive, Mike. Are you disciplining him?"

"That would be my business."

"It would also be Mr. Wiltern's business. I intend to phone him, if I don't get a satisfactory answer from you."

"Do what you have to do, busher. I have a club to run and no time for meaningless chit-chat." I hung up.

The phone rang again. I didn't answer it. Myrna finally did, and told me it was Briggs.

"Tell him I'm in the shower and will call him back."

She relayed the message and replaced the phone. She looked at me worriedly. "What's going on, Mike?"

"This year, we are going all the way."

"False pride goeth before the fall, Mike."

"That's a misquote. I'll see you Sunday night."

We were three games in front of Baltimore and five in front of Boston. They had not done in September what they had in August, when they had played against a string of losers.

We would play three at Detroit, three at Milwaukee, and then come home to finish the season, our first lucky scheduling break of the year.

Algernon would be getting itchier and itchier on the bench. We would have his stubborn spirit and alert bat out there before too long.

He stayed stubborn. We stayed lucky. Detroit set a club season record for errors in the opener and we took advantage of most of them. Every had room for mistakes, but made very few. I will not reveal the score in print, not wishing to rub salt in the wounds of my many readers in Detroit, but you could write and ask them, if you have friends or relatives there.

Lepert lost the second game, thanks to Stark trying to surpass the new Detroit record all by himself. Spack re-established our obvious superiority in the third game. We were still five in front of Boston, three in front of Baltimore.

On the plane to Milwaukee, Heinie reminded me, "This is September. We could bring Caravelli up from Oil City."

"I've already sent for him," I said. "That might help to soften Ward's attitude, too. The kid might remember he has no guaranteed job in the big time."

Heinie chuckled.

"All right," I said. "*All right!* Does everything I say have to make sense?"

Our thin-ice starter did a Jekyll-Hyde in the opener against Milwaukee, precision pitching all the way, a performance that matched the classics of his Cy Young year. Mel had been right about him. Caravelli was a step up from Stark, but by no means a Ward. Pulaski had been right about him.

Every lost a heartbreaker, putting two on in the eighth, before I sent in Miller. The two on were Every's responsibility and Miller let them come home on his first pitch, giving up a triple to May.

Jess pitched the Sunday afternoon game under a hot Milwaukee sun, knowing the importance of it, dredging up everything he had ever learned about the men he faced and their vulnerabilities. Leeds took over in the seventh to save it for him.

We had taken two out of three from the Brewers—and lost a game advantage to Baltimore, who had to be playing over their heads. They were two behind, Boston six.

We would close out the season against Cleveland and Baltimore; there was no way now we could finish worse than a tie for second with Boston. That was only a mathematical extrapolation; it was also true that Boston could finish in a first place tie with us—if we hadn't been playing Baltimore. They were mathematically out of title consideration, and knew it.

That could make them lose, I figured, when they met Baltimore, the club they would play before coming to New York. Baltimore would be tight, needing the wins.

These are the mathematical shenanigans that infiltrate your thoughts in desperation month. A man has a second-division mind if he relies on his competitors to do his work for him.

We had the edge; all we had to do was win. Who wants to back into a title? All right, I'll be honest. I'll take a title any way it's delivered.

"Good road trip," Myrna greeted me, Sunday night. "But Baltimore's gone crazy."

"I noticed. But they have three with Boston and Boston's had good luck against them all year."

"I'll make you a sandwich," she said.

I went out to the kitchen with her. "I suppose there's been a lot of static in the local press about Ward sitting on the bench?"

"Some," she admitted. "Did Briggs phone you on the road?"

"No. Why?"

82

"He phoned again right after you left, Monday. He sounded very disturbed."

"He probably phoned Wiltern after that and Wiltern told him to go back to emptying ash trays. If he phones here, you can tell him I'm in Madagascar."

She was slicing some cold turkey now, but evidently not ready to talk it. I knew there was something on her mind.

She brought me a sandwich, loaded with white meat, and a bottle of beer. She sat down across from me.

"You're thinking about Ward," I said.

"And not kindly," she admitted. "I think he's being very unreasonable. And over-loyal to Jimmy. I mean, after you explained about the five phone calls, and all—" She shook her head. "He's being unfair, Mike. You are totally in the right on this."

"He's a bull-headed rookie," I said, "but he'll come around. I did not explain about the five phone calls to him, nor the visit to his room. That was a rather obvious fishing expedition, Mrs. Ryan."

She nodded thoughtfully. "I get less subtle as I get older. I suppose not interfering lately has made me rusty."

"And not interfering in this will insure our domestic harmony. Is there more turkey?"

Boston would be loose against Baltimore and Cleveland would be almost as loose against us. They were heading nowhere. There was a reason to believe they would like to knock us out of it, no doubt, indulging in the fantasy that they, too, would be contenders if they'd had Bernardi.

I didn't want any final day dramatics, where the last man comes up with two out in the bottom of the ninth, the bases loaded, and hits the heroic homer that wins it for the good guys.

We had the strongest, soundest club in our division. If we

couldn't close it out before the 162nd game, my critics would be right—I didn't deserve to be the manager of the New York Titans.

Spack opened the Cleveland series. The game could have been called, after the third. But I suppose the nine-inning rule is in the book so the vendors can sell more hot dogs and management can waste energy on lights.

We had a six-run lead at the time. No team ever fielded in the history of the game was going to pick up six runs on Elmer Everett that night. He allowed two hits and one walk (intentional), lowering his earned run average to 1.97.

Caravelli came up with two key hits. Ward squirmed on the bench each time. The girls in Oil City are not as pretty as the girls in New York, nor as plentiful.

Baltimore had lucked out against Boston, taking advantage of three Red Sox errors. We still had the two-game lead and only five to go.

Cavanaugh reversed his Jekyll-Hyde characterization in the second game. It was his philanthropist night again, awarding hits and walks to all the Indians weakened by the famine of the night before.

"I still say he needs Ward out there," Red said.

"Keep saying it, Red, and it will become your epitaph."

I sent in Balding, then Leeds. To no avail. Their ball game.

But Boston had come up with four runs in the eighth to edge Baltimore, 5 to 4. We still had the two-game advantage.

Every pitched a beauty for us next night, throwing a five-hitter at them, holding them to one run, despite two errors by Caravelli. Baltimore had used Palmer with only two days' rest behind him, a desperate gamble. Palmer had come through with the win, but how could they now use him against us?

We had a two-game lead with three games to go. The nights had been cold and were not due to change. Leppert was next in rotation.

"What do you think?" I asked Red. "We could open with Dorn again and trust the bullpen."

"Jess would like to start," Red said. "He told me so. I suppose it's not a time to be sentimental, is it?"

"No. But it might be time to listen to a mature, wise, and self-knowing professional. We'll go with Jess."

I gave the boys a short talk before we went out to face Cuellar, pointing out the obvious, which is quite often necessary with ballplayers.

"We need only one of the three," I told them. "Any one of the three might be sufficient for you healthy youngsters. But I, as most of you veterans know, have a weak stomach. I do not believe it can hold up beyond tonight."

I looked directly at Ward when I used the word "youngsters" and he looked directly at me, in his fearless way. Time would soften him, as it had me. I had been as ornery as he was, when I was his age.

Jess gave us five of the smartest, guttiest innings I had witnessed in a long, long time, using his arm, his brain, his memory, but mostly his heart. We supported him with two doubles and three singles for two runs.

Before the sixth, he told me, "That's it for me, skipper. I don't want to be known as the man who lost us a flag."

"And I don't want to go down in history as the man who ruined your arm, Jess. There are too many years ahead when we will need that arm. Thank you for what you did tonight."

I was lying, and he knew it. Old folks lie to each other, softening the gloom of the twilight years.

Balding went in—and gave the two runs back in the sixth. It was probably too hot a night for a man who had spent so much time in California, almost 53 degrees above zero.

Leeds held them scoreless through the seventh and the eighth. We, too, came up with nothing. Leeds still looked strong, finishing the eighth, but now would be a bad time to erode his new confidence. He was still a rookie, and the Cleveland power was due up in the ninth.

Bernardi pitched the ninth, smiling, strong, and able, rendering their power powerless, a man who needed neither the playoff nor the Series money, only the sustenance of challenge. He knew what he had to do; the bottom third of our order was due up in the ninth, and we had a tied ball game.

Caravelli led off. He topped a little trickler down the line and streaked toward first, as though racing toward the closing doorway to the majors, which he might have reasoned it could be. He beat the throw.

Heilbraun went up and laid down a perfect bunt, sacrificing Caravelli to second.

And now Luther? Luther had a lifetime batting average against Cuellar of .087. I looked along the bench, seeking a pinch hitter.

I looked at Ward and he looked at me. Then he smiled and stood up and came out to where I stood, at the end of the dugout.

And in front of fifty thousand people, about 99 percent of them readers of Rusty Jones, he held a ten-dollar bill aloft for all to see—and brought them to their feet, cheering.

"You are one great showboater," I said, "but I here and now, in front of these cheering thousands, rescind the fine."

"I have been carrying this bill in my uniform for two days," he told me, "waiting for the appropriate time. Don't call it a fine. Call it payment for five phone calls, at two dollars a call."

86

I took the ten. "Go out there and hit one," I said, "and bygones will be bygones."

He walked to the plate and Red came over. "Should I help Voltz warm up? Keller's off his feed."

Keller was our second-string catcher, Voltz a rookie from Oil City.

"No need," I told Red. "This is the last inning, and the winning run on second will soon be home."

"You and your hunches!" he snorted. "I'll warm up Voltz."

Voltz never got his gear on. Ward disdained the first pitch—and knocked the next one out of the park.

9

At home, I told Myrna, "There was a miracle tonight, out at Titan Stadium, and nobody in the stands realized it."

"I was there," she said. "I didn't see any miracle."

"In the bottom of the ninth," I explained, "a boy came up to me and told me something that only two people in the world knew, before he told me. I call that a miracle."

She said nothing.

"He handed me a ten-dollar bill," I continued, "and said it was to pay for five phone calls. You and I were the only people in the world who knew about those five phone calls. The kid must be psychic."

She said levelly, "I have never in my life talked with Al Ward, either by phone, or face to face."

"Do you occasionally phone his roommate?"

"Jimmy is a friend of mine. Just because he is not a friend of yours does not mean he cannot be a friend of mine."

"Did you by chance mention the five phone calls?"

"I chided him in a motherly way," she admitted, "about

gallivanting around Milwaukee when you were trying to reach him. Do you want to play some gin rummy?''

Oakland had sewed up the Eastern Division crown. The Dodgers and the Giants were two games apart in the National League West. That could be settled tonight, while I was relieving Myrna of some of her household money. St. Louis had already won the National League East.

We had two meaningless games with Baltimore still to play. I used the boys from the bench, giving them some action in competition that might stand us in good stead through the trials to come. I worked all our pitchers, a couple innings here, a couple innings there.

Oakland was undoubtedly going through the same routine out there in Birdland West. They had been the first club in ten years to win two World Series in a row. In order to win their third, they would have to get into it—over us.

Among all of them, the Dodgers shaped up as our worthiest possible foe. They had hitting, pitching, speed, the gloves. They had the great brain of Walter Alston. Injuries had hurt them early in the season, so the Giants had still been contenders in the last week. That had ended three hours after we had clinched our flag, Los Angeles winning the decider the same night.

If this seems as though I am downgrading Oakland, I have given you the wrong impression. They were a great team. But we had beaten them eight times this season and lost to them only four. One would have to assume we were a greater team.

''I won't be going to Oakland,'' Myrna informed me. ''Sheila and I are playing in a duplicate bridge tournament in Yonkers. I'm sure you can handle Oakland without me.''

''I think I can handle it alone. The sad part is you'll be missing a visit to the Golden State.''

"Sheila and I will get out there," she said, "when we play the Dodgers. And if you need help with Oakland, there's always the phone."

Little domestic jokes, to brighten the hearth and home. . . . Though you can never be sure when Myrna is joking.

We had come a long way from fifth place. I received a congratulatory telegram from C. F. Wiltern, full of glowing praise I am too modest to record.

I could not have done it without the boys, of course, or the fine coaching staff. And Myrna had contributed, too, filtering out the hate mail, the obnoxious phone calls, running an efficient household where a man could find quiet and peace, necessary for thinking. No man can do it alone, even Mel King.

Mel, of all people, was at the airport!

"What gives?" I asked.

"I heard Myrna wasn't going," he said, "so I rushed to your aid. I may no longer be an official member of this club, but I have my loyalties."

I stared at him.

He laughed. "Relax, Mike. The AP has commissioned me to cover the club from here in. I am now a writer, and will soon be as famous at that as I was as a player, and later a manager."

"Most of the writers I've read were also big readers. You were never that, Mel."

"You read the wrong writers," he said. "I'll be writing for the newspapers."

"That's different," I admitted. "Sit with me on the plane and go over the Oakland roster with me. There are less than a dozen men in the world who know more about baseball than you do."

He sighed. "It was only three or four in January. You will have me back in the minors before you're through."

He sat with me, but we didn't talk about Oakland much. We talked about our heroes mostly, the bigger-than-life men who had made headlines in the first half of this declining century. Don't get me wrong; there are plenty of stars in this half. There just don't seem to be any heroes.

I voiced this thought to Mel.

"Performance makes stars," he told me. "The public makes heroes. We are living in a disenchanted time, Mike."

That was pretty perceptive for a non-reader. Maybe he wasn't. There are secret drinkers; he could be a secret reader.

We were six miles above Utah when he said, "I didn't leave you much, did I? Spack is about all."

"And Oliver and Valdez. It took a few years to rebuild."

"You did a beautiful job. I guess you know how much I hate these flying machines?"

"I've been wondering about that," I admitted.

"The Associated Press," he told me, "doesn't have enough money or enough borrowing power to get me on one of these, if I didn't want to be here. I want to be with you when you finally come into your own. Nobody respects you more than I do, Mike."

"Thank you," I said. "It's mutual. It must be comforting to be retired, so you can say what you really think."

He nodded. "People seem to be starting it earlier, these days. Maybe that's why we don't have any heroes."

You open with Spack and split the next four, and you are ready to go into the Series. That is one way to figure. Spack had not lost to Oakland in four years.

You open with Spack and follow with Cavanaugh, and hope Cavanaugh is lucky. Then you need only one win in the next three games to sew it up, all of them at home.

They would all be day games, so there would be no need for earmuffs or hand-warmers. This silly thought hit me. You open with Dorn and make them nervous, then bring in Bernardi. Tony can pitch two innings in the time it takes Lem to adjust his cap. Wouldn't that be a change of pace to throw at the champions of the Golden West?

Silly thoughts a man has. . . . I am no computer-programmed robot. I follow my instincts, play my hunches. But over the long season, baseball is a percentage game; you go with the stats and follow the book.

I would open with Spack. This was not the minors, where a man could have some fun. Ring Lardner had named it right—we were heading for the World Serious.

The plane went into its glide pattern, slanting down toward Oakland. Mel's knuckles were bloodless, gripping the arm rests. His safety belt was buckled so tight, I'm surprised it didn't cut him in half.

But I had sat next to a man once who had been even more frightened in a landing pattern—and learned later he was a transcontinental pilot.

The Oakland A's had three pitchers who had won 20 games or more this season, Holtzman, Hunter, and Blue. They had also lost some games, a number of them to us.

Hunter was the only right-hander in the trio and had the best won-lost record, though the highest earned run average. They would open with him. Spack had beaten him, 2 to 1, in July and not faced him since.

We were favored to win the opener, according to the prophets who put out the morning line. These odds were probably calculated off our season record against them. One thing the crystal ball boys overlooked was that the A's had been here before, their third playoff series in three years. It was our first, under me.

Spack had been in playoffs under Mel, and so had Valdez and Oliver. They had won a World Series, under Mel. Heilbraun had been in plenty of playoffs at Baltimore. Ward? A green rookie at showdown time? His arrogance would carry him through it.

The sun was shining in the Oakland-Alameda County Coliseum. The place was jammed. Through their years here, the A's attendance had not kept pace with their success. That would change, as the new fans were converted from the lesser sports.

Spack looked ready. So did Hunter. Our average was better against right-handers; the two southpaws who would follow Hunter should give us more trouble.

Hunter gave us enough, striking out Valdez and Oliver, getting Davis to ground out. Valdez strikes out about once a decade; I had an uneasy feeling.

Spack faced four batters before getting the last out. It didn't seem to me as if his fastball was moving, or his curve breaking enough. I asked Luther.

"I've seen him pitch better," Luther said. "But he often starts slow. I don't know what to tell you, skipper."

There it was, hunch against stats again. You have to stay with the record, with only one inning gone.

Hunter mowed down three more without strain in the second. Spack gave up a hit and a walk, no run. I looked at Red. Red shrugged.

Tied at zero, you might be thinking: What's the old man fretting about? It was not the score. It was this uncomfortable feeling I had.

Perry Washington opened the third with a single, our first hit. Heilbraun bunted him to second—and Luther struck out. Valdez came up, the smartest bat in either league, and struck out for the second time in one game, a record for him.

Catfish Hunter had gone through three innings with one hit and five strikeouts. The pattern was forming in my mind. He was on, today, a hundred percent on. And Spack was below his best. He would need his best to match Catfish today.

Bando knocked one out in the fifth. Green and Tenace combined to get them another run in the seventh. There was no point in relieving Elmer. Even though he was less than 100 percent, we had no reliever to match him. Giving up two runs through seven innings is not exactly poor pitching.

They were never threatened. Hunter was in total command from his first pitch. Their ball game, through every inning.

We had played the defending champions of the world and lost. It was possible our boys might have wondered, during the night, if our season's dominance of the A's had been a fluke. Hunter had made it look too easy.

Before they went out next day, I told them, "What you saw yesterday, you are not likely to see again. It was one of the best pitched ball games I have ever seen, and I've been watching them for forty-six years. You won't see another like it this year, either from Oakland or any other club we will face."

All of my pitchers had been rested, as had Oakland's. They would go with Vida Blue. I asked Red about Cavanaugh.

"The only choice," he said. "We need to take at least one win out of here." He grinned. "And we don't want to disappoint all those Green Bay Pirate fans who will be watching on the tube."

There is a time for humor and a time for gravity, a distinction Red frequently fails to observe. "Okay," I said. "You made the decision."

"I hope it's the right one," he said. "Sheila is still talking Bermuda."

94

Vida started the second game as though he were trying to make a liar out of me, breezing through Valdez, Oliver, and Davis as easily as Hunter had yesterday.

Cavanaugh walked the first batter—and then settled down. He was *on,* today. At least 90 percent of his adolescent speed was back. Mel had been right in January; he had learned to think. And my harsh words had not gone unheeded; he had learned to trust Luther.

We went through three scoreless innings without any need for stomach tablets. Lover boy was off and winging. Mel would be basking in self-admiration up in the press box, but that was okay. Cavanaugh was making us both happy.

"Old Red was right, as usual," old Red said. "The kid must think he's still back in St. Louis."

In the fourth, Valdez steered a single between second and short, and Oliver walked to the plate and looked at Heinie for the signal. My hunch was too strong to ignore. Hit away, he was told.

He lined a leg triple into the right-hand corner. We had our first run of the series.

"The way Cavanaugh is pitching," Red admitted, "I never would have called that."

"Even old Red is not infallible," I said. "I want our boys to get their confidence back."

Kermit Davis came up and hit a bloop double that brought in the second run, and brought in the Oakland pitching coach to the mound. Rollie Fingers came in, bringing his waxed moustache along.

He had an earned run average of 1.92 for the season and usually gave us more trouble than any pitcher on their staff.

He gave up the hit to Paige that brought Davis home. It was shaping up as a laugher for us, three runs in and nobody out. There were still only three runs on the board when Perry

Washington fouled out, leaving Paige at second.

Jimmy had room for error now. I would have to watch him closely. He and his roomie had a tendency to relax when ahead, neither being horizon scanners by nature.

Red had guessed right. Jimmy continued to pitch as if he were still trying to prove he was the rising star he had been before his fall. He gave up one walk and one hit and won it, 4 to 0.

They were noisy in the locker room, but I called for order. I told them, "I lied to you boys earlier today, and hereby apologize. I guaranteed that you would never see another performance this year to match Hunter's of yesterday. You have just seen it surpassed by our own James Cavanaugh. I am telling you the obvious, but wish to go on record as making the statement."

Applause and laughter. Jimmy smiled and Ward smiled, but neither applauded nor laughed. The unforgiving stubbornness of youth. . . .

10

"Wasn't Jimmy spectacular?" were Myrna's words of greeting.

"He certainly was. How did you fare in Yonkers?"

"We finished second. Sheila was not up to par. You know, when I was watching Elmer lose that heartbreaker, I had this silly thought. What if you had opened with Lem Dorn, and then brought in Tony? Think of that for a confusing contrast to throw at the A's!"

I had sent her a picture postcard from Oakland, but never mentioned that. I said quietly, "We have been together a long time. We are finally of one mind."

"You thought of the same thing?"

I nodded. "On the plane, riding with Mel. He's a writer now."

"I heard," she said. "Mike, we *are* one mind. You mustn't fight it."

"Your IQ of 147 plus mine of 93 would still average out

to well over 100," I admitted. "I will give it serious consideration."

"The Dodgers are in, aren't they?" she asked. "St. Louis will be no match for them. It could be over in three."

They had taken two from the Cardinals at St. Louis. I said, "They're the best in that league, without question. I think we're a stronger club, because of our bullpen."

She nodded. "I agree. Would you like something to eat? I'm hungry."

Cal Every for the third game? He, too, had been in playoff games, with Pittsburgh. But his record against the A's? Of the four games we had lost to them this season, he had lost two, one to Holtzman, one to Blue. The whimsy hit me again—Dorn, followed by Bernardi. It had worked in May, against Kansas City.

May games are important, playoff games more so. I decided to stay with the tradition. I would start Every. He had lost both games by a combined total of three runs, 2 to 3, 0 to 2. The boys had not been hitting in either game.

Holtzman was the man he would face. Cal had lost to him; he had also bested him, getting a lot of help from our bats. The bats had come to life against Blue. There was no reason to assume they would die young.

There is only one major defect in Cal as a pitcher; he has this mistaken belief his fastball is a sizzler. That belief is probably the reason we had been able to get him from Pittsburgh.

He opened with it to the first Oakland batter, Campaneris. Campy punched it into right field. Locust went out to tell Cal what he must have been told a thousand times before. Cal nodded in his polite way, undoubtedly reserving his own opinion on the subject, as all pitchers do.

98

Rudi came up and hit into a double play, letting me breathe again. Bando walked to the plate with two gone and nobody on. Luther went out to warn Cal once more and Cal nodded once more. Sal Bando is not a man you overpower.

Cal got two strikes quickly enough, one foul, one called. Two pitches missed the plate, and then a third. Three and two to Bando.

Red muttered something.

Cal shook off the first call, and Red muttered again.

Cal delivered—and we were a run behind, with two out in the first. The ball was caught by a kid who had brought his glove to the game, deep in the cheap seats.

"I'll talk to him," Red said.

"Watch your temper," I warned him.

"I was thinking of yours," he said. "That's why I'm going out."

Red's words must have found a home. Cal threw everything but fastballs at Jackson and ended their half of the inning.

"Pitchers," Luther growled. "All pride and no brain, that's pitchers."

I had crouched behind the plate for twenty-four years with the same thought. I said, "It's no time for dissension, Luther, but I must privately admit you are right."

Valdez worked a walk out of Holtzman, fouling off every pitch not to his taste, waiting for Holtzman to run out of patience. Oliver laid down the intended sacrifice bunt along the first-base line. Tenace overran it. Two on, none out.

Kermit Davis' triple brought them both home and gave us a one-run edge. The first third of our order had been more successful through the tail end of our season than our muscle boys. Holtzman went through Paige, Ward, and Willie

Washington without putting them on base. But Ward's long fly ball had brought Kermit home. We had a two-run lead at the end of the first.

Cal was not right. He stumbled through a couple of innings, putting runners on base, being saved each time by our classy infield.

The A's were beginning to look tight and impatient. They had come up with too many hits to be behind. Cal wasn't that good today, and they knew it.

The whimsy hit me again. What better time? I sent Dorn in to open the fourth inning.

"You're a complicated man," Red said. "I wish I could follow your thinking."

I made no comment.

Lem looked around, counting the house. The attendance figure was on the board, but he might have suspected they had missed a fan or two. Then he studied the resin bag, as though it was a long lost artifact, and slowly swiveled his head to make sure the bases were empty. He took a minute or two with his cap, adjusting it exactly right for the TV cameras—and finally peered in at Luther for his sign.

"We'll be late for dinner," Red said. "Did you bring a sandwich?"

I shook my head.

Davalillo was the batter; he had been in and out of the box a half dozen times, waiting for Lem. He swung at the first pitch, though it had bounced a foot in front of the plate, and we were off for three innings of slow motion baseball.

Our honorable opponents began to use their noodles in the seventh, waiting for Lem to bring one into the strike zone. I'm not sure if Lem knows where the strike zone is, though he has pitched for many years.

He walked the first two in the seventh—and I changed the

format of my whimsy, bringing in Leeds instead of Bernardi. Tony knew where the strike zone was; he lived there. But the Oakland power was due up and Leeds was trickier than Tony. He worked us out of it with one run. Titans 3, A's 2.

He edged the corners and kept changing his pace, keeping them off balance. They caught onto his rhythm in the ninth. Bernardi went in, with a runner on first and one down.

He didn't use many pitches, just enough to save the ball game for Lem. Two games to go, and we needed to win only one of them.

"When great minds agree," Myrna said, "even when they are three thousand miles apart—"

"I used our original two-man scenario in May against the Royals," I informed her. "You may have listened to the game on the radio between bridge hands."

"It's possible," she agreed. "Jess tomorrow?"

"Unless you disapprove?"

She said nothing, looking abused.

"I apologize. Jess tomorrow," I said.

We had picked up Jess from the Phillies three years ago. That meant his total experience in playoff games had been as a spectator, either on the tube or in the stands. He was still my best choice.

Myrna was unusually quiet at dinner, and I asked her why.

"You seem tense," she said. "I thought a little quiet might be restful for you."

"It's World Serious time, Myrna. I want us to be in on it."

"We will be," she promised. "Sheila and I have given it an exhaustive analysis from all angles. There is no way we can miss."

"I wish you had told me earlier. It would have dispelled my doubts. How about some gin rummy tonight?"

"It's the least I can do," she said.

The Dodgers had edged the Cardinals, 2 to 1, wrapping it up. They would have plenty of time to rest their pitchers before the Series. They would be some mountain to climb. First we must earn the right to start climbing them.

Jess is one of those men who was born looking old and adds to it, through the years. He may have put on a little extra age overnight; he looked weary, warming up. I mentioned it to Red.

"It's possible he didn't get much sleep," Red said. "When you spend your working years with the Phillies, you don't experience the heavy tension of playoff time."

"We'll stick with him," I decided.

He threw everything he had, including his heart, at the Oakland batters, like a wrinkled boy with his thumb in the dike. He kept them contained for three innings. The A's had come back with Hunter, knowing they wouldn't need him tomorrow if they didn't win today.

His skill matched Jess' heart and we had three scoreless innings.

The water began to leak through in their half of the fourth. Rudi walked and Green doubled him to third. I sent in Balding, to keep the leak from becoming a flood. Rudi came home on a long fly out by Tenace, but Balding held the damage to one run.

A one-run cushion shouldn't have stood up against our bats. Hunter, with ninth inning help from Fingers, made it stand up.

It was a quiet locker room. The boys were probably wondering what I forced myself not to wonder. Was Hunter that good or were we in a hitting slump? Hunter was good, but *that* good?

Tomorrow, my ace. He had pitched a sound game at Oak-

102

land and lost it. If our bats were as cold as they had seemed to be today, Spack would need to pitch a better game tomorrow.

I kept dreaming and waking up, dreaming and waking up. The dreams had nothing to do with baseball. I don't even remember what they were about now, only that they were the kind that wake you up.

The morning was damp and overcast. There was a sixty percent chance of rain, the weatherman predicted.

"You're not eating," Myrna told me. "At least drink some milk, Mike. Should I warm you some?"

"I guess. I might keep it down. I am really worried about our hitting."

"The A's must be worrying, too," she pointed out. "They only came up with one run, and they weren't facing Elmer or Jimmy."

That was true. I said, "We're better than they are."

"As they will learn today," she agreed. "Don't forget to save Mary and Harvey some Series tickets."

"They can use Wiltern's box," I suggested. "He probably won't be using it."

The weatherman was sixty percent wrong, qualifying him to become a baseball writer. The sun came out around eleven o'clock.

Elmer Everett looked strong. Bugs assured me the slight muscle pull he had suffered at Oakland had responded to treatment. When you go with your best, and fail, you have done all you can. Nothing is as futile as regret. That is the sensible way to look at it. It would be a long and bitter winter for me, however, if we did not win today.

None of the staff had any jibes; they were as grim as I was. Even Ward looked serious in the locker room.

Fun in the sun on the grass, that is traditional baseball.

They had taken away our sun for most of the games and given us lights. They had taken away our grass and given us synthetic turf. They had expanded both leagues and sold out their traditional heritage to the TV networks and the absentee owners.

They couldn't spoil the grandeur of the World Series. We were one game away from showdown time in America.

Elmer stood on the mound and smiled absently at all his infielders, no doubt reaching down into his Columbia-trained mind to recall the mistakes he might have made in Oakland, the strengths and weaknesses of the batters he might have overlooked.

Luther held one clenched fist aloft in salute, and settled behind the plate.

Zip! Called strike. Lazy curve, inside corner. Swinging strike. Elmer tried to waste one then, but Campaneris wouldn't let him, swinging at an outside pitch. The A's, too, could have been wondering about yesterday, when they had come through for only one run against an aged pitcher.

"Are those stomach tablets any help?" Red asked.

"Probably not. Mental, mostly, probably."

"Give me one," he said.

Elmer started to blow them down. Vida Blue continued to hold us scoreless.

"Elmer's using his speed too much," Red complained. "He's making it personal."

I agreed. Elmer had the whole arsenal. The speed of a pitcher that fully equipped is often overlooked by the so-called experts, but he had it. No matter what you might read about the old-timers, no pitcher can rely on his blazer through nine innings. Elmer must have resented his loss at Oakland, his first there in four years.

Jackson guessed right in the fifth and blasted one out of the

104

park, heading for Wall Street. Red went to the mound to remind Elmer of his other ammunition.

It was 1 to 0, middle of the fifth.

We almost came back in our half. Ward led off with a single and Perry Washington hit a low screamer into center field that should have gone for a double. But Reggie Jackson dove and caught the ball a foot above the ground. Ward got back to first in time to beat the throw.

We were still alive, a man on and only one out.

Heilbraun advanced Ward to second with a single. Then Luther came up and hit one down the third-base line that had "run batted in" all over it. But Bando made a miracle catch, and caught Ward off base, for the third out.

There was very little harsh noise in the stadium, just the sound of fifty thousand people breathing heavily. I thought I heard the *thumb* of somebody pounding a bat on the floor of the dugout. Nobody was moving around in there; it was my heart.

Elmer had thrown too hard through the early innings. He began to tire in the eighth, walking Fosse. I sent in George Leeds.

He had come of age. He gave the hungry Oakland batters everything but what they were looking for and ended the inning with Fosse still at first.

Blue was going strong. He faced four men in our half of the inning and got three of them, leaving one on.

Leeds got the first two batters in the ninth. Tony went in to get the third, though the man was 3 and 0 when Tony took over. Oakland on top, 1 to 0, middle of the ninth.

There is a time to live and a time to die. Our time was growing short, three outs short of being dead.

One of the local cliché-addicted scribes had named Algernon "The Blond Bomber" in this morning's paper. The noise from the stands increased as he walked to the plate.

He acknowledged the applause with a busher's tip of the cap and faced Blue with the innocent arrogance of youth.

Vida made him look bad with a curve, which the kid missed by a foot. And then Vida's own inherent pitchers' arrogance turned the tables. He tried to steam one down the middle.

Ward was on second before Jackson could get the ball there. Perry Washington was due up. I looked along the bench.

But I decided to stay with Perry, as Myrna had convinced me I should, two years ago.

It turned out to be one of my better decisions. Perry took one low for a ball, one inside for a strike—and poled the third pitch high in the center-field stands for the American League Championship.

11

Myrna greeted me at the door with a kiss and a hug. "Welcome home, major league manager of a champion."

"We've had a great year," I said, "so far. Our toughest test still lies ahead."

"They could be the second best club in organized ball," she admitted.

"And maybe the best?"

"That's negative thinking, Mike."

What would I do with Kermit Davis? There would be no designated hitter in the Series, the idea not having been accepted by what is haughtily referred to as the senior circuit.

Over cold snacks and a bottle of Einlicher in the den, I wondered aloud, "What will I do with Kermit Davis?"

"You'll have time to think about it, Mike. You have two days of rest before the Series starts."

"Our infield is solid," I pointed out, "and so is our outfield. There is no place anywhere in the lineup for Davis, except as a pinch hitter. And his bat cools off if it's not used every day.''

"If the Dodgers are as strong as the writers claim," she said, "his bat may be needed every day."

That was a thought, but not a comforting one. If I had to use Kermit early in a game, I would lose some great gloves. There are positions in the outfield, depending on the pitcher, where a great glove is not needed. But all my outfielders were hitting well, including Perry Washington. Our center fielder, Otis Paige, was batting cleanup.

Nit-picking, all of this, tilting at trifles. We had the pitching. We had the hitting (playoff games excepted) and we had the gloves. If the Dodgers were better, luckier, or better managed, they would win. And vice versa.

They could be better managed, with Walter Alston, but you must remember my modesty when you judge that statement.

We would open at home for two games, go to Los Angeles for three (if needed) and come home for the final two (if needed). In the last twenty years, more than half of the Series had gone the full seven games, including the last three. Most of the men who knew gave us the edge in pitching. In a seven-game Series, pitching is a big edge to have.

My ace had started two games in the playoffs, lost one, won none. Cavanaugh had started one game and won it. But a man has to be judged over the season, and Spack had been my stopper all year.

Two days rest was not enough, however; I would open with Cavanaugh against Los Angeles.

They would open with a well rested Don Sutton. Their starters were equal to (or better than?) ours. We had a stronger bullpen. Their club batting average was slightly higher than ours. Our slugging average was well above theirs, as was our run production. They had Walter Alston, whom I have mentioned before.

You go with your ablest men, handle them as well as you know how, and accept what comes, good or bad. These are noble sentiments to express to youth groups in lectures during the off season. Let me go on record as admitting I do not lose graciously.

The weatherman came through for the opener. The temperature at game time was almost 68 degrees, with no breeze, slightly overcast.

Charles Frederick Wiltern had jetted back from Rome for the Series, but there was plenty of room for two more in his box. So Mary and Harve had their choice seats for the ridiculous things that happened that day.

About the only pleasant thing about the game was that I developed a new respect for the patience and forbearance of Jimmy Cavanaugh. And Don Sutton. Their teammates were in the stadium with them, but had invented a new game, to be played without pitchers.

The first man up, Lopes, hit an easy grounder to Heilbraun—and my heady, steady Kraut threw it into the dugout! Joshua hit a lazy blooper that Ward went out and waited for—and dropped!

I had a feeling right then we were in a fall rerun of the 17 to 16 debacle in Florida in April. I forget what Wynn hit, or even if he hit it. I know they finished their half of the inning with four runs, not one of which was officially earned.

Was I going to relieve a pitcher who was pitching no-hit ball? Would you?

Sutton was smiling as he took the mound. A four-run cushion in the first inning; he had reason to smile. He had a season era of 2.21 and could now pitch the way he wanted to, not the way he needed to.

It really didn't matter how he pitched. Valdez rolled one to Russell, the best shortstop in their league. Russell picked it up four times before he found the handle. Valdez was on second by that time.

Oliver swung at a third strike, missed it by a foot, and Ferguson, the best young catcher in either league (except for Johnny Bench), let the ball get by him and roll to the backstop.

"What is this game?" Red asked. "What is it called?"

I had no answer. It was their game, not mine. I was not eligible to play in it.

The score was 4 to 3 at the end of the first inning, on a total of one hit by Willie Washington. If you want stats absurd enough to match the game, score it one half-hit for each side. There is no way it resembled an official game, requiring its own rules.

There had been a full moon the night before and a few of the local loonies later attributed it to that. I am a rational man and have no explanation to offer.

It was 8 to 7, Dodgers still on top, through the sixth inning. Both starting pitchers had gone out for pinch hitters by this time. Both had pitched well. Both must have wondered why they had taken the trouble to learn their trade.

Tony was going for us now. The way I saw it, if the batter doesn't make contact with the ball, there is no way an infielder can handle (and bobble) it. If nobody gets on base, nobody comes home. This is very primitive thinking, of course, but in newly invented games, the strategy is often primitive.

Ferguson came up in the eighth and made contact with one of Tony's blazers. Dodgers 9, Titans 7, middle of the eighth.

Ron Cey mishandled a ground ball in our half and Valdez

110

reached first safely. On the mound, Brewer looked annoyed. I played the hunch, sending in Keller to bat for Oliver. Keller hits about one pitch out of eight, facing cool pitchers. Brewer did not look cool at the moment.

Keller took a little extra time getting ready to bat, scratching out a canyon for his right foot, examining his sculpture with an artist's eye before making sure it was deep enough. Then he went back to get the pine tar for the handle of his bat. A .237 hitter must use his other weapons.

Brewer was now steaming. So was his first pitch. Keller knocked it into the second deck and we had a tie score for the first time that day.

Brewer recovered his cool; we opened the ninth with the same score, Leeds on the mound for us.

Showdown time in a crazy game is no place for a nervous rookie. Cey doubled and Wynn brought him home with a long single. Balding went in to close out their half of the inning.

A one-run lead in a game this absurd was not impressive. There wasn't too much reason to be disheartened.

But apparently the Dodgers had become bored with the new game. They went back to baseball. Grounders that would have gone for doubles through the first eight and a half innings were suddenly outs once again. There were three grounders for three outs almost as quickly as I record them here.

We were a step further from the World Championship than we had been this morning.

What do you tell your boys? They must play better tomorrow? They knew that. I told them nothing, as silent and furious as they were. One thing was sure, the errors could not cause dissension; they had *all* committed them.

Myrna, too, had no words, just a sad smile.

Around nine o'clock, I said firmly, "Tomorrow will be better."

She nodded. "Elmer will make it a sane world again."

I didn't read the sports pages next morning, realizing what fun vitriolic writers could have reporting yesterday's farce. I stayed with the brighter news—murder, poverty, rioting, and war.

Spack would make us healthy again, I told myself on the way to the stadium. Spack had had bad luck in the playoffs, but this was the money time and he was a money pitcher.

My usually wordy staff had few words today, possibly still suffering from shock. "Spack will even it for us," I told Red.

"We hope. I don't want to leave town two games down."

"Win or lose, you'll still have your Bermuda money when it's all over."

"It's not a time for grim humor, Mike. We looked *bad* yesterday!"

"We made one less error than they did," I said. "I hope the local sports experts pointed that out in their columns this morning."

"I didn't read 'em. I'm going to check with Bugs on that muscle pull of Elmer's."

He left me and I stood there, watching the early arrivals arrive. Mary and Harve were already in Wiltern's box. I went over.

"How come you didn't eat dinner with us last night?" I asked my darling daughter.

She glanced at Harve and shrugged.

Harve said, "Myrna thought it might be a bad time."

"Why? You win some, you lose some."

Mary looked at me worriedly. "Daddy, are you all right?"

112

"I'm in a World Series. How much righter can a man be?"

"I suppose. Elmer's going to do it for us today, isn't he?"

"I guarantee it."

There are no guarantees, in life or baseball. You take the best available boys you can assemble and get them into condition and . . . I guess I have mentioned that before.

"Why are you smiling?" Heinie asked. "Somebody tell you a joke?"

"It is my brave smile," I explained. "I am like the clown who is dying inside. I owe it to my boys and our many fans to smile in the face of adversity."

"You can quit now," he said. "You're making me nervous."

Elmer was smiling as he warmed up. He might have been looking ahead to the fall hunting season, his favorite off-season sport. But I had a feeling he knew what I did.

"Everything okay?" I asked him.

"I've never been readier," he said. "I will give you ten dollars for every hit they get if you will give me ten for every strikeout I get."

"The odds are wrong," I told him, "but thanks for the offer."

If we had given him support, it would have been an easy first five innings for Spack that afternoon. Fielding support, we gave him, a 180-degree reversal of our performance yesterday. Though our bats weren't cold, they were colder than the Dodger gloves.

He and Messersmith went through five tight innings of scoreless, errorless ball. Each pitcher had given up two hits through the period, but Spack had a big edge in strikeouts, 7 to Messersmith's 3.

It was still scoreless in our half of the sixth, when Valdez

113

lined a double into right field. Oliver advanced him to third on a deep infield groundout. Ward came up, batting where Kermit had in the American League season.

He wasn't smiling. I can't remember that he had smiled since the playoffs began.

He had learned patience. He worked Messersmith up to 3 and 1 before he found a pitch he liked. Once he had found it, he hit it, deep into center field, rolling toward the wall. Valdez was in the dugout and Algernon at second before the ball came back to the infield.

As Otis walked to the plate, I handed my package of stomach tablets to Red. "It's going to be a laugher," I announced.

"Keep your pills," he said. "You could need them later. I'll just take a couple."

Otis banged one against the fence and the laugher was under way. Rau came in for them—and soon left, followed by Richert.

Two outs and five runs later, I asked Red, "Was I right?"

"If a five-run lead is a laugher, you were right."

"The way Elmer's pitching?"

"You were probably right."

It was 5 to 0 through the sixth, 5 to 0 final. We were breathing again. Now, if we could pick up a quick three in Los Angeles, I wouldn't need the stomach pills until next spring.

The foregoing is hyperbole, I hope you understand. You do not "pick up a quick three" on Walter Alston.

Mary and Harve came over for dinner before heading back to Passaic. Myrna spent most of her time packing for her three-day visit to Los Angeles. She and Sheila and Rose Schultz would fly out there first class in a 747, courtesy of our young owner.

114

This would deprive the coaching staff of badly needed amateur advice during the trip. We would have to sweat out our own strategy.

Mel sat with me again. "I am paying you the ultimate compliment," he reminded me, "riding in one of these doom-buggies. You must not fail me, Mike."

"It depends on the boys," I said.

"It always does. But they're *your* boys."

"Miss it, Mel?"

"I do. Though I'm ashamed to admit it. Eighteen years with a gastric ulcer that finally went away when I settled in Connecticut. What kind of fool would miss a gastric ulcer?"

"Our kind, Mel. We're a vanishing breed."

"No," he said. "Never!"

He was a stubborn man. Winners frequently are.

Walter Alston was a stubborn man, too, and a winner. He had a habit of staring off into space, a middle distance look, even when he was being interviewed. Managing the Dodgers through all those years, he must have seen some strange happenings on the field. His remote look could have been caused by shock or wonder.

With the travel day off, I could still use Spack and Cavanaugh in Los Angeles. The Dodgers could use Sutton and Messersmith again. Tomorrow, I would go with Cal Every, the Dodgers with Claude Osteen, a southpaw, a soldier who had been to many wars.

Neither was very impressive that sunny October afternoon in The City of the Angels. Both were trying to be too precise, shading corners—that they both missed.

It was 0 to 0 through the third, thanks to the two tightest infields in organized ball. It was not a pitchers' day. It was a glove day.

In the bottom half of the fourth, Cal decided it was the

115

proper time to try his semi-fastball. Cey illustrated the fallacy of his thinking by lining a homer into the left field seats. Dodgers, 1 to 0, end of the fourth.

"Claude's outpitching Cal," Red said. "Though neither really looks sharp."

"I know. Maybe, we can outluck 'em."

Cal gave up two hits for a run in the sixth, and I relieved him with Balding. Osteen had settled down now, getting stronger and sharper. Balding matched him through two innings. We started the ninth still short by two runs.

Balding was due up; he would not come up. I had already used Kermit Davis in the fifth. That left me a choice between Keller or Wallace. Keller's batting average was 10 percentage points higher. He went up to face Osteen, looking determined.

He came back to the dugout five pitches later, looking disgusted.

Valdez tried to chop one between first and second—and was nipped at the bag by inches, a doubtful call. Oliver lined a long out to Willie Crawford. We had taken another backward step.

Myrna had a beloved cousin in Pacific Palisades, and we went out there for dinner that night. Pacific Palisades is officially Los Angeles, but seventeen miles from City Hall. The cab fare was only slightly less than my share of the playoff money.

Though Myrna's cousin was a sweet woman and an excellent cook, her husband was something else. Basically, he had two things wrong with him; he was an engineer and a Dodger fan.

Over the hors d'oeuvres, he explained to me why the Titans could not become the Champions of the World, laying

116

it all out in engineer prose, position by position.

"Did you figure this out on your slide rule," I asked him, "or trust the feelings and instincts which God bestows on all, including engineers?"

"I used the company computer," he explained. "I'm sure you are not prepared to argue with a computer?"

"I am not inclined to argue with anybody who has a wife who cooks like yours," I said, "but if you have some loose money lying around, and are prepared to put your money where your computer is, I will be happy to cover it."

"Scientific men," he explained loftily, "search only for truth, not monetary advantage."

"I have a rookie shortstop with the same belief," I said, "and I must respect his opinion. Because even you must admit he is superior to Bill Russell."

"Nobody in the world, in or out of baseball," this objective, scientific man said, "is superior to Bill Russell!"

That great brain had more than he deserved or had earned in life, a wife who could cook.

On the ride back to Myrna's hotel in Beverly Hills, she asked me, "Jimmy tomorrow?"

"Yes."

"He's worked out, hasn't he?"

"Yes."

"Why did you use Keller instead of Wallace this afternoon?"

"Because his pinch-hitting average is ten points higher than Wallace's. Stick with the bridge, Myrna."

"Yes, dear. Are we going to make it?"

"We are going to make it."

I kissed her good night at her hotel and moved with the cabby closer to the smoggiest part of town, wondering why

117

she had mentioned Keller and Wallace. Did she know something I didn't? How could she? She had never worn a baseball uniform in her life.

Jimmy, according to Red, had gone to bed at nine o'clock. It was now eleven, and there were still a few athletes around the lobby—until they spotted me. Eleven o'clock here was two in the morning back home. But today's athletes are like engineers; they put their trust in clocks and computers, not what their natural instincts tell them.

For the second day in a row, the sun was out next morning, a Los Angeles record. Mark Button and Pete Pulaski were sitting in a booth in the grille with Mel and they waved for me to join them.

"Not if I'm buying," I said. "I have had previous experience with Pulaski's appetite."

"Would we invite you to join us, if we expected you to pop?" Mel asked. "You must learn to trust people, Mike."

"And pay your just dues," Mark added. "Who signed Ward for you? Whose wife gave you the tip on Balding?"

"I'll buy," I said. "You boys must have known I was only joking!"

The way they laughed at that, you'd think I had said something funny.

I was attacking my first egg (and Pulaski his fifth) when I said, "I am sitting here with three of the greatest baseball minds extant. I would like, in all humility, to ask a question. Who would you have brought in to pinch hit yesterday in the ninth, Keller or Wallace?"

"Same as you," Mel said. "Keller hits southpaws better than Wallace."

"And has more experience than Wallace," Pete added.

"And ten full points more in batting percentage," Mark

118

said. "Has some second-guesser been giving you static on it?"

"Nothing like that," I said. "It was just one of those dark doubts a man harbors in the long night."

I had no idea what the club had paid to get Balding and Ward, but they now cost an extra twenty-seven dollars, the breakfast tab for gluttons.

The Golden Boy in the Golden State, the handsome male lead in his natural Hollywood environment; he had the setting for his starring role that afternoon and the cast to support him.

We gave him hits, we gave him gloves, we made him look better than he was. I am not belittling the man; he pitched a solid game. To the trained eye, Sutton was pitching a better one. They hit grounders to our gloves. We hit grounders with eyes, grounders that took crazy bounces.

Sutton went out for a pinch hitter in the sixth and Rau came in to open the seventh. We had a 2 to 0 lead at the time. We extended it to 5 to 0 off Rau and Richert.

Ferguson and Lopes got doubles in their half of the inning to bring them one run closer, but the Cavanaugh magic held up. He went all the way for the win. The two best clubs in baseball were again peers.

And tomorrow, Spack. The dreams weren't bad that night, not even bad enough to remember.

The weather had gone back to normal, overcast and chilly. It was the kind of weather that could aggravate a lingering muscle pull, but Bugs and Red assured me Spack was fit and ready.

Messersmith obviously did not intend to lose two in a row to our ace. He dispatched Valdez, Oliver, and Ward with a minimum of effort, three short fly outs off eight pitches.

Spack did not look quite as ready as I had been told. The first two batters he faced worked him all the way to a 3-and-2 count before he could set them down, one strikeout, one long fly ball. The third batter, Wynn, bounced a single into center field.

Ferguson came up, batting cleanup. Spack respected him too much, finally walking him. And now Russell. I looked at Red. Red shrugged.

Russell took a pitch inside for a ball—and really tagged the second one, soaring toward the left-field fence.

If it had been a few inches higher, we would have been down by three runs. But Perry Washington leaped higher than I knew he could, juggled it on the tip of his glove, and held on to it for the third out.

I asked Luther what he thought.

"I think he's going to be all right, skipper. Especially, if we can get him a couple of runs. He threw a lot of pitches for one inning, though."

I nodded. He would bear watching.

Paige opened the second for us with a smashing double that bounced off the base of the center-field wall. Messersmith looked mildly surprised, though not disturbed. Willie Washington was smiling as he walked to the plate. He smiles quite often, but I have learned to distinguish between them. This was his confident hitter's smile.

It was possible Andy Messersmith did not relish seeing that kind of smile on a batter so soon after he had given up a double. He threw his swiftest and his best.

It was swift enough, but not best enough. Willie was on second and Otis home a few seconds later.

Walt Alston walked slowly to the mound with his middle distance look. He walked slowly back a little later, leaving Andy on the mound.

120

Perry Washington came up. He, too, was smiling, a rarity for him. He had imitated Willie with that circus catch; maybe he thought using Willie's smile would keep his luck going.

Andy stared at the smile and turned around to see the same smile standing at second. Andy was frowning, starting to think a little harder. He walked Perry, still thinking, and Heilbraun stepped up to the plate.

Carl Heilbraun hits between one and two homers a year. He had already hit his quota for this season, two. This had to be his banner year; he hit the second pitch along the line, a foot inside the left-field foul pole, for our four-run lead. Brewer came in for them.

The Dodgers do not quit. They kept getting men on base, trying to nibble away our lead with singles. It was 4 to 2, middle of the eighth, and Elmer had thrown too many pitches by that time. I sent Bernardi in.

His fastball was not the fastest I had ever seen him throw, but it was considerably faster than Elmer's had been in the last few innings. He pitched us through the eighth without damage.

We came up with a walk and a hit, but no runs, in the ninth. They would send up men in the inning who generally murder fastballs.

"Leeds?" I asked Red.

"Why not Leppert?" he suggested. "He's earned his right to tell his grandchildren about his day in the sun in the Series."

"He has no grandchildren, to my knowledge," I said.

"He will have. He has two daughters. But will he ever again have a chance to pitch in a World Series?"

Leppert had very little experience as a bullpen pitcher. It is a highly specialized trade, requiring unique skills. But he was cunning and he was brave and he was always ready.

121

"Leppert it will be," I decided. "I hope you have guessed right."

"I hope so, too. I took the liberty of calling the bullpen five minutes ago and telling him to warm up."

As if I hadn't noticed. . . . I made no comment.

He did all of us proud, that old tiger, mostly himself, in the last inning. He threw pitches at those muscular youths they had never seen or read about. More fox than tiger, I guess you would have to say, but enough of both to send the hungry young lions back to their cage, whimpering.

Our own young lions mobbed him after the third out, but I finally got to him to tell him, "This could give us new hope for next year, Jess."

"It doesn't matter, Mike," he told me. "I've had my day."

12

Six miles high and heading for the Paris of America in a noisy plane. We were a game up on the National League Champions and recording it in song and laughter.

"I wish they would cut down the decibels," Mel said. "I worked in a plane factory during the Second World War and there were plenty of rivets we didn't flatten too good. A racket like this could loosen them."

"I doubt if many of those planes are still in service, Mel. We're going to make it, aren't we?"

"New York, you mean? I sure as hell hope so!"

"The World Championship, I mean. I want to follow in your honored footsteps."

"I hope you do," he said. "But first we must get to New York in a shivering plane. You coming back with Every?"

"Who else? Two days of rest is not enough for Cavanaugh, and Spack pitched today."

He said nothing.

"Speak your mind," I said.

"Cal's okay," he said. "You figure the booze has weakened Jimmy by that much?"

"Even a lifetime teetotaler would have trouble with the Dodger bats after only two days of rest," I pointed out. "Aren't you the man who always played it by the book?"

"Not always. I occasionally trusted my hunches. But it's your club now, Mike, not mine."

It was probably the hilarity in the plane that had affected his thinking. Come back with Cavanaugh?

Myrna had arrived earlier on the commercial flight, but waited for me at Kennedy. In the bus, she said, "We are only a step or two from the end of the glorious season, aren't we?"

"Mel thinks it should be one," I said. "He more or less suggested I use Cavanaugh."

"After only two days of rest—?"

"My feeling exactly. Mel is getting old, and there was a lot of distracting noise on the plane. The reason I came back tonight instead of tomorrow was to use our travel day for the pause that refreshes."

"You're not going to work the boys tomorrow?"

"Only a couple of hours. They have earned their respite."

"It's already tomorrow, Mike," she said. "It's two o'clock."

"It will be an afternoon workout," I explained.

The boys didn't really need the practice or the calisthenics. They were in shape and they were sharp. But it is not healthy for young minds to loll around hotel rooms, worrying about tomorrow. By getting them outside and active, they would have less free time for brooding.

I would go with Every. He was my third best, admittedly, but he was rested and he was experienced and he was professional. If tragedy befell us (a loss), Spack would be rested enough and ready for the last day decider, if Cavanaugh faltered. Every pitcher on the staff would be standing by that day.

Osteen would face Every. His win over Cal in Los Angeles might help to make him confident. But yesterday is not today, as I have explained before, nor this week last week.

As it turned out, Osteen did not beat Every. We picked up a run on him in the second inning, two more in the third. When he walked the leadoff man in the fourth, Alston came in with the hook, replacing him with Brewer. He got three outs without damage.

We had a 3–0 lead and a veteran pitcher on the mound who had finally learned his fastball wasn't. Cal Every had given up only two hits and one walk through four innings.

"His pitching or their bats?" I asked Red.

"A little of both. They've swung at some bad pitches. This game means more to them than it does to us. They have to be overanxious and guessing."

With a pitcher like Spack or Bernardi, you have to guess. Bernardi's fastest is faster than the eye and Spack's brain is better than the batter's. With Every, a batter can wait, and they probably weren't.

Alston had a little talk with Buckner before he came to the plate in the sixth. Buckner waited—and finally walked, their second walk of the game.

Ferguson stepped up to the plate, strong and young and brave and smart.

"Could I have one of those tablets?" Red asked.

I gave him one and took one.

Ferguson disdained the first pitch, a slow curve for a called strike. He rejected the second, an outside pitch below the strike zone. The third pitch was another curve ball—which didn't curve enough. Fergy hit it into the bleachers and our lead was down to one run.

Applause shook the stadium, for these were the former Brooklyn Dodgers, playing in the most forgiving city in the world.

I walked very slowly toward the mound, to give our bullpen time. I stopped about halfway and rubbed my brow, started back toward the dugout, and then turned around again.

"Let's go, Mike," Sid Gomer, the plate umpire, came out to tell me. "You're not that indecisive, despite your age!"

"That remark," I promised him, "will be recorded in print when this game is over and mailed special delivery to the Commissioner."

"I'm shaking in my boots," he said. "Move it, Mike!"

I glanced toward the bullpen, where Balding was warming up. I said, "There is no room for insolence in baseball, Sid. I'm shocked that a man who has earned the great honor of umpiring in a World Series should have so little respect for the hallowed traditions of the game."

"Save your corn for the winter lecture circuit," he said grimly. "Any more yak out of you and you will see the rest of *this* game on the boob tube in the locker room."

"Huh!" I said, and went to the mound.

"They were lucky," Cal said.

"You think you're one hundred percent?"

He paused before he answered, so I didn't listen to the answer. I glanced toward the bullpen once more, started toward the dugout, came back, and pretended to be having a heart-to-heart dialogue with my pitcher.

All the umpires came over, and our infielders. Luther walked slowly out from his position.

126

"You've got four seconds, Mike," Sid said evenly. "One—two—three—"

I signaled for Balding to come in.

He gave up a scratch hit, no runs, and our big bats came up to face Brewer, planning to add to our cushion.

Jim Brewer's plans were at a variance with ours, of course, and he prevailed temporarily, rolling the ball around in his glove, as is his habit, studying each batter as though he were a bug on a pin, allowing one walk but no hits through four batters.

"He's good," Red said. "He's sharp today."

"He can be had," I said. "Positive thinking, Red."

"I am a positive thinker. But it has never carried me to the point of self-delusion. I'm glad we have the one-run cushion."

We didn't have it long. Jimmy Wynn, the Toy Cannon, came up in the seventh with two out and a man on second. He tied it up with a blooper that dribbled off the edge of Ward's glove, halfway to the outfield. It had really been Perry's ball, but who can fault a man for trying too hard?

I sent in Tony. He ended the inning with four pitches.

Brewer continued to read minds and fool bats. With two out in our half, I sent Kermit Davis in to hit for Bernardi, a bad move. This was a mind Brewer could read in braille. Three pitches gave him the third out.

Vance Miller opened the eighth for us, getting the first two without trouble, having too much trouble with Crawford, who finally walked. The Dodgers, through the season, had been the best two-out scorers in the game. Red mumbled something I can't put into print.

Mota came in to hit for Paciorek. Leeds was ready in the bullpen, but I decided to stick with Vance, my second consecutive bad move. Mota lined a double inside Oliver that

127

wouldn't quit rolling. Crawford slid home on a close call at the plate. For the first time that afternoon, we were behind.

We stayed there. Brewer was too much for us that day, and I had made some bad guesses. We had played 173 games of a rewarding season. The big reward was still a game away.

"Tomorrow," Red said.

"Tomorrow," I said.

But who could be sure?

"Tomorrow," Myrna said, at home.

"That was our big word during the busher years," I reminded her. "It was always tomorrow, when I would be up where I belonged again. But tomorrow will soon be today and maybe I am a man from yesterday."

"You're the greatest, Mike, and we both know it. Stop that kind of talk!"

"Does the greatest bring in a mind like Kermit's to face a thinking pitcher like Jim Brewer?"

"It was not a thinking contest. Kermit is a better hitter, I'm sure, than Brewer is a thinker. Though I don't read as much as I used to, I doubt if there are any learned essays carrying the byline of James Brewer. Kermit was your only possible choice."

"You're probably right. Even if you aren't, thanks."

Sutton, tomorrow. He had won that crazy first game, having gone the necessary five innings. He had lost to Cavanaugh in Los Angeles, going five. If he lost tomorrow, his Series record would be one win and two losses. Though the Dodgers were a generous club, it didn't seem likely they would pay a pitcher $113,000 a year to lose two out of three.

But in two games, he had survived for a total of only ten innings; rack that fact up on our side, negative thinker.

I might not be the greatest, but *we* were, as the world

128

would learn tomorrow. This was my dominant thought at bedtime.

"Sleeping pill?" Myrna asked.

"The stomach pills are enough. I don't want to turn into a dope fiend."

The sun came up hot and red next morning. Dorn, followed by Bernardi . . . ? Of course not! Cavanaugh, the man Mel had suggested I pitch yesterday.

Cavanaugh on the mound and every available arm standing by. It was not probable that Brewer would be standing by for them; he had pitched too many innings in the Series. That was all right with me.

The boys were quiet in the locker room. I didn't have any words for them. They knew what I was thinking; they were thinking the same. There are times when a man need not vocalize the obvious.

"Everything okay?" I asked Jimmy.

He nodded.

"You should have won that first one, too," I said. "There is no way that could be called a game of baseball."

"It's history," he said. "Today is all that matters."

It was a bright, hot day. There were no clouds overhead and the few on the horizon were small and motionless and far away.

Heinie and Rose wanted us to go on a trip to Germany with them this winter. Win or lose, we would go. I owed Myrna a change of scene. My knee throbbed with a twinge of pain. I wondered where Gud Filcher was now, and if he still had headaches from our collision.

"You're looking too gloomy," Heinie said. "I prefer that idiotic smile you displayed before the second game."

"It's the World Serious," I said. "It's the one hundred and seventy-fourth game of a long season. I'm tired."

129

"It's better than counting money in a bank," he said. "Ask Tony. It's been a great year, Mike."

Yes, it had been. How could a rational man put so much importance on one game after a season like ours? By this time, you must know I am not a rational man and never intend to be. We have a country currently run by supposedly rational men. I rest my case.

The $113,000 pitcher looked sharp to me. I asked Red for confirmation.

"No sharper than Cavanaugh," he said. "What are we paying Jimmy?"

"A lot less than we will next year, no doubt. Brewer isn't going to be available, is he?"

"Probably not. Just Messersmith and Tommy John and Downing and—"

"Enough!" I said. "Spack healthy?"

"One hundred percent."

The fans stood for the Anthem, except the fans in one section, reserved for our crippled war veterans. How many had come home crippled and how many were we honoring today? Some world the rational men had given us. . . .

Jimmy stood on the mound, a man who had made a bad guesser out of me. He didn't smile, he didn't fidget, he didn't argue with Luther. He pitched.

He pitched like a Cy Young, MVP, Rookie-of-the-Year pitcher, all of which he had been. Three up, three down.

Sutton wasn't smiling, either. Three up, three down.

Through the second, the same. Through the third, ditto.

"Have two pitchers in the same game ever pitched no-hitters?" Red asked.

"Not within my recollection. Are they both that good, or am I missing something?"

"If you're missing it, so am I. They are *hot* today!"

130

Valdez broke the spell in the fourth, lashing a vicious triple down the line. A man on third and nobody out; almost anything would bring him home.

Nobody came up with anything, not today, against Sutton. It was 0–0, end of the fourth.

In the sixth, they broke our spell, a single from Buckner, a double from Lopes—for the run. I went out to the mound.

"I'm okay," Jimmy said. "I got careless. That's their last run."

"I believe you," I said, and went back to the dugout.

In our half of the sixth, Ward doubled and Otis brought him home. The clouds on the horizon were still small and motionless.

Alston took his big gamble in the seventh. With a runner at second and Sutton due up, he sent in Manny Mota to hit for him. Walter doesn't make many mistakes and this couldn't qualify as one.

Mota hit the second pitch so hard I could feel the shock of it through the ground beneath my feet. Perry Washington went racing back, the ball well over his head. One millionth of a second before it dropped over the fence, he leaped and caught it.

Tommy John came in to pitch the bottom of the seventh, a left-hander who had frequently made us look bad in exhibition games. We didn't improve our image in the seventh.

"I'm getting too old for this business," Heinie said. "My heart won't take it."

I said nothing.

Jimmy faced four batters in the eighth, walking one, striking out two, getting Joshua to hit an infield pop-up.

With two gone in our half, John walked the next two and Alston went out to talk with him. He left him in, the right decision. Perry fouled out to end the inning.

Jimmy was picking up his glove when I told him, "You must be tired."

He shook his head.

"Not vanity, Jimmy?"

He shook his head again. "I've outgrown that. I promise you they won't get another run off me."

They got what the scorer called a hit, the only man in the park who saw it that way, a slow roller that Heilbraun didn't charge, letting the ball play him. Buckner stood at first, looking hopeful.

I didn't need to watch Jimmy; I could tell how the game was going by watching the hope drain out of Billy Buck's face. I watched Jimmy, though, enjoying an artist at his work. It was 1 to 1, middle of the ninth.

Heilbraun, Locust, and Jimmy were due up for us. Carl's bat hadn't been too hot in the Series, but he had been here before and would not panic. I took a chance. He must have fouled off a dozen pitches before he fouled out.

Tommy John would be too much for Luther, the way I saw it. Kermit Davis went up to hit for him. Our regular season designated hitter came through, lining a bouncer into center field, legging it into a double.

And now who? Another dilemma. There are very few problems in baseball I cannot handle, but dilemmas are my weakest category.

Vern Arch, the plate umpire said, "Let's go, Mike. Get a man up to that plate."

"I plan to," I said.

"Now!" he said.

Wallace or Keller? Keller or Wallace? The same dilemma I had faced in Los Angeles. From one corner of my eye, I saw a sheet of waxed paper flutter down from a box seat.

"One moment, Vern," I said. "There is nothing as slippery as waxed paper and the park is full of valuable athletes. I will be back as soon as I pick it up.''

''The bat boy can handle it,'' he said.

''I need the exercise,'' I told him. ''Patience, Vern. It will all be over soon enough.''

I went over quickly, but bent over slowly, as old men often do. I couldn't be sure the waxed paper had dropped from Myrna's hot dog, but there was none around the sandwich she was holding.

''Keller, of course,'' Sheila was saying. ''He hits left-handed pitching better and is a full ten points higher than Wallace in average.''

''You are failing to look at the entire picture,'' Myrna informed her, ''just as you did at Yonkers. Against left-handed pitchers in *afternoon games* in the *late innings,* Wallace is hitting almost eighteen points better than Keller.''

When I went back, Vern said, ''You've had it, Mike!''

''Had what? Didn't you hear me tell you Wallace before I went over? Is it too much to expect you could tell him while I was trying to prevent a serious injury?''

He glared at me. ''Okay. But don't think you're fooling me. If this wasn't the Series—''

Wallace went up to the plate, taking his time.

''What goes on?'' Red asked.

''Nothing important. It was just that Sheila wasn't seeing the entire picture. Nor Mel, nor Pulaski, nor me, nor Button.''

''Have you gone bananas? What are you talking about?''

''What do I always talk about during working hours? Baseball, Red, that's all.''

''It must be the sun,'' he decided.

Wallace looked at a fastball, low, and a slider, outside. Two balls and no strikes to Wallace, but he wasn't up there to walk. Tommy John must have thought he was; he put one over the plate.

Wallace hit it between second and short. For all I know, the ball is still rolling. We were the Champions of the World!

The boys had wasted all the champagne, pouring it on each other in a youthful display of conspicuous consumption. They were quieted down now and when I came out to meet Myrna at the club-house door, there was still some network time between commercials they had to fill in. It had been a fast game.

Windy Earnest Allsell stood there with a few cameras they didn't need for commercials.

"And here he is," Windy announced to his unseen audience, "the undeniably astute manager of the Champions of the World, along with his charming wife, Myrna. Exciting series, wasn't it, Mike?"

"Satisfactory," I admitted.

"And you, Mrs. Ryan," he went on, "are known throughout this great city as one of its most gracious hostesses and efficient homemakers. I'm sure Mike will admit you played your important part in today's triumph."

"You would have to ask Mike about that," Myrna said modestly.

Windy looked at me, ignoring his producer's signal for a cutaway.

"I would be less than candid," I said, "If I did not here and now in front of your millions of viewers publicly admit I could never have done it without her."